Katie, Bride of Virginia

American Order Bride Series Book 10

By Sylvia McDaniel

Books by Sylvia McDaniel

Contemporary Romance

Standalones
The Reluctant Santa
My Sister's Boyfriend
The Wanted Bride
The Relationship Coach
Her Christmas Lie
Secrets, Lies, and Online Dating
Paying for the Past
Cupid's Revenge

Anthologies
Kisses, Laughter & Love
Christmas with you

Collaborative Series

Magic, New Mexico
Touch of Decadence

Western Historicals

Standalones
A Hero's Heart
A Scarlet Bride
Second Chance Cowboy

The Cuvier Women
Wronged
Betrayed
Beguiled

Lipstick and Lead
Desperate
Deadly
Dangerous
Daring
Determined
Deceived

Scandalous Suffragettes
Abigail
Bella
Callie
Faith

The Burnett Brides
The Rancher Takes a Bride
The Outlaw Takes a Bride
The Marshal Takes a Bride
The Christmas Bride

Anthologies
Wild Western Women
Courting the West
Wild Western Women Ride Again

Collaborative Series

The Surprise Brides
Ethan

American Mail Order Brides
Katie

Katie, Bride of Virginia
Published by Virtual Bookseller

Cover Design by Erin Dameron Hill
http://edhgraphics.blogspot.com/

Edited by Tina Winograd
www.tinaeditservices.com

Formatted by Laurelle Procter
laurelleprocter@gmail.com

Short Description: Is it only coincidental that the damage to Daniel O'Malley winery coincides with his mail order bride's arrival?

ISBN: 978-1-942608-57-8 (paperback)
ISBN: 978-1-942608-09-7 (e-book)

{Victorian Historical Romance – Fiction}

www.SylviaMcDaniel.com

Synopsis

Katie, Bride of Virginia, is tenth in the unprecedented 50-book American Mail-Order Brides series.

A disastrous factory fire ends Katie Maverick's livelihood and she must find something quick. Convinced to become a mail-order bride, she receives an offer of marriage from Daniel O'Malley.

Only Daniel isn't the one who put the ad in the Grooms' Gazette. His business partner, secretly placed the ad in Daniel's name. When Katie arrives, a surprised Daniel agrees to marry her with the idea she could help make his life easier and still the gossip surrounding the death of his wife.

He's unprepared for the way the bubbly girl from Massachusetts eases his loneliness. Not only is she helpful, she's breaking through the walls he's erected around his heart. Troubled by the suspicious vandalizing suddenly occurring in the vineyard, Daniel wonders if things might not be as good as they seem. Is it only coincidental that the damage to his winery coincides with Katie's arrival?

Could this sweet, innocent woman and his dead wife share a common goal to destroy him?

Table of Contents

Chapter One

Katie Maverick dodged a horse and buggy as she ran across the busy street in Lawrenceville, Massachusetts, hurrying back to the grungy apartment she shared with two other young women. The unopened letter in hand could be the answer to her prayers, or the start to her demise.

Since the fire had destroyed the factory where the three had worked, they'd made the decision to find husbands, and signed up as mail-order brides.

Julia and Genny were leaving at the end of the week for their new lives with the men who'd responded to their letters. And Katie couldn't afford the apartment alone.

Unable to bear if the news was bad, she waited to open the letter with her friends for support.

After running into the small, over-packed building, she threw open the apartment door. Genny stood at the stove, mixing cornbread for the third time that week for supper. "Good, you're home. Cornbread and milk is about all we have to eat."

Katie held up her envelope. "I think it's a response to my mail-order letter."

"Julia, come in here," Genny called. "Katie has her letter."

Julia, came around the corner of the one bedroom they all shared. "Open it. What does it say?"

With shaking hands, Katie ripped the seal on the envelope that held her future. She glanced at her friends and licked her lips, her heart pounding in her chest.

"Dear, Miss Maverick, I'd like to offer to marry you."

Katie squealed with excitement, her friends joining her as they all jumped up and down. She had an offer of marriage.

"Oh my God, you did it," Genny said.

"Read the rest of the letter," Julia responded.

"As my wife," the girls tittered again, "you will be expected to help my aging mother and take care of the house. I live ten miles from Charlottesville, Virginia and own a vineyard which is the family business.

"As your husband, I will provide for you, though I'm not wealthy by any means. If this arrangement is agreeable to you, I have enclosed a train ticket from Lawrence to Charlottesville.

Please telegram my friend, Frank Lowe the details of when and if you will arrive. I look forward to meeting you.

Sincerely, Daniel O'Malley."

Katie's heart leaped in her chest, she was getting married. The three girls squealed again, and came together in one big hug as they jumped up and down, until Julia had to stop because of pain in her leg. All three had found husbands.

"You can leave right away, so you don't have to pay the apartment rent," Genny said relief in her voice. "I was so worried about you."

Julia hugged her tightly. "And you're getting married."

Katie laughed and swept back her long hair. "No more working in a factory."

"A vineyard. Maybe your husband's wine is sold where we live. Every time I see a bottle, I'll think of you. Wonder what the name of his vineyard is?" Julia asked.

For weeks they'd each anxiously awaited letters, hoping they wouldn't have to find another job in a factory or resort to cleaning houses. Katie squeezed her eyes shut and crushed the letter to chest. She sighed, fighting back the tears. Her mother would have been so pleased that she found a husband.

Since the factory fire left them without jobs, their situation appeared hopeless until a friend, had convinced them to send off letters to prospective grooms. Now they were all going to be married.

"Two more days together and then we each leave. Genny to Nevada, Julia to New York, and me to Virginia. We're spread across the country at different ends. I wish we were closer. I'm thrilled we've all found husbands, but I'm so sad to be leaving you," Katie said.

"We'll still be friends," Julia said, reaching out and patting her on the back.

"Yes, we'll write each other," Genny, the practical one of the three said. "But still it will be sad not living together."

"We should celebrate," Julia said. "Let's go to the cafe and have dessert."

Katie grinned. "We haven't been there since the fire. What do you say, Genny?"

"Let me grab my coat."

~

Daniel O'Malley rode into Charlottesville in his sidebar buggy. He almost brought his mother with him, thinking the outing would be good, but Frank, had been insistent he come to town today.

And he feared Frank, his business partner, would tell him what he already knew: the vineyard was in trouble. Three years had passed and still the wine had to ferment. Occasionally he would uncork a bottle and check the taste, but the batches needed longer. More time to chill for the taste to explode on the tongue. Soon, hopefully soon.

Since the death of his first wife, he'd avoided coming into town and wouldn't have come today, except Frank's note said it was urgent.

Pulling the buggy to a stop, he jumped down and tied the reins to a hitching post. When he walked into the office, he tipped his hat to the woman behind the desk. "Hello, Mr. O'Malley, Mr. Lowe is expecting you. Go on back to his office."

"Thank you," Daniel said as he walked past the woman.

When he stepped into his best friend and business partner's office, Frank glanced up from the paperwork scattered across his desk. "You came. Take a seat."

Sitting on the other side of the desk, Daniel gazed at his friend wondering about his message. "Of course, you said it was urgent."

"It is," Frank said, staring at him. "I may have overstepped the boundaries of our friendship."

Daniel frowned. Frank had helped him when the vineyard needed money. Friends since college, there wasn't much he wouldn't do for Frank and doubted the man had done anything offensive. "What did you do?"

"I ordered you a mail-order bride."

For a moment, Daniel sat stunned. "What?" The memory of his last wife was still too painful to think about and Frank had found him a mail-order bride. Was he crazy?

"A wife. You need a wife, Daniel, to help with your mother. To keep your house and even help with the business. You're alone and after what happened to Eloise, I feared you would never even look at a woman again, let alone marry. So I ordered you a mail-order bride."

What was he thinking to find him a wife? *He* didn't want or need another woman. And yes, his mother needed someone to nurse her, but not at the expense of him marrying again.

His fists clenched. "You're right. You did overstep the boundaries. What makes you think I would even *consider* marrying again?"

Frank leaned back in his chair and studied his friend. "You need help with your mother for one thing. How can you take care of her and work in the fields? Plus, I think the best way a man can rebound is to find someone else."

"I don't want anyone else. I never want to marry again."

Anger coursed through Daniel like a river at flood stage. They were good friends, but this was too much. Frank knew better than to bring a woman into Daniel's life.

For a moment, Frank didn't say anything. "A woman is arriving on the noon train today from Lawrenceville, Massachusetts. She thinks you ordered her."

"Then I suggest *you* marry her or you send her back, because I'm not getting married."

Frank sighed. "Fine, I'll send her back. But what can it hurt to meet her? What if she's gorgeous? What if she could give your mother the care she needs and you could devote all your time to the vineyard? What if she helped the people in town forget about Eloise?"

Daniel stared at his friend. He hadn't even looked at another woman since his first wife's death. In fact, he'd thought he would forever be a widower. The nights were lonely at the vineyard and his mother did need help, but then again, marry in haste and repent at leisure. No, he wasn't getting married again.

"It couldn't hurt to meet the train and see this woman? Could it? Then, if you don't think it's a good match, we'll put her on the next train back to Lawrenceville."

"I'm not getting married."

This trip into town had been a total waste of time. He had much more urgent things he should be doing, but he still needed to take care of this problem. He didn't want word getting out that he "neglected" another wife. Frank was going to apologize and explain everything to this woman.

"Of course you're not getting married. We're just going to meet the train."

"You can express your regrets to the woman, saying you made a terrible mistake and pay for her return ticket. It's the least you can do," Daniel said knowing no lady wanted to be Daniel O'Malley's wife.

The woman had come all this way, and he knew what it was like to be misled, scorned, and turned away. He would meet the train with Frank beside him, her return ticket in hand, apology on his tongue. This had gone far enough. Daniel would never marry again.

~

Katie gazed out the train window, a warm glow filling her. Lush oak trees, as far as the eye could see backed by the Blue Ridge Mountains, soothed her battered soul. A chill nipped the air, and she realized though traveling south, the weather didn't feel any different. But still the winters couldn't be colder than the frigid state where she'd been born.

Before she left, she'd made one last trip to the graveyard to say goodbye to her mother and father and siblings. Everyone was gone, but her. She'd been alone these last six years, first living in the orphanage and later working at the factory.

Mr. Bob Brown, the factory owner, told the sisters at the orphanage that he was giving these girls valuable training and education that would keep them off the streets. He'd made them more like slaves, working them twelve to fourteen hours a day until the time he set the factory on fire.

With a sigh, she glanced at the houses and buildings as the train pulled into Charlottesville. This was a new beginning. A new start and she was determined to greet her new husband with a smile. There was nothing Katie Maverick couldn't overcome, nothing.

She was the only surviving member of her family from a yellow fever epidemic. The sisters at the orphanage had reminded her she was strong and blessed, and to live each day grateful and happy. And so far, even during the darkest times in the factory, she reminded herself she was blessed. She was alive.

The train stopped and the conductor opened the doors. She searched the crowd and tried to imagine which man, waiting on the platform, was her future husband. Butterflies filled her stomach and she stood, her hands shaking. The woman beside her smiled. "Good luck."

"Thank you," she said. "Maybe we'll meet again sometime."

"Maybe," she said as Katie walked toward the door that would change her life forever.

She stepped into the bright sunshine, breathed the fresh air and lifted her face to the sun. She'd made it out of Lawrenceville. With a smile she walked to the edge of the platform where two men were standing, watching her.

Tilting her head, she wondered at the men. One of them had dark features, with a strong jaw and blue eyes the color of an iris in springtime. He was so strong and manly and handsome that her heart skipped a beat.

Halting for a moment, she watched as they walked towards her.

"Miss Maverick?"

She smiled, suddenly feeling so very blessed if that dark, striking man would soon be her husband. "Yes, Mr. O'Malley?"

The second man, the one less handsome laughed. "I'm Mr. Lowe, this is Mr. O'Malley."

A ripple ran through her at her man. It was him. The man with the deepest blue eyes she'd ever seen, but a smile didn't grace his face. In fact, he almost seemed kind of a sourpuss.

The man took a step closer, his eyes assessing her and then he bent over and kissed the top of her hand like a gentleman would do. She could almost hear the breath in her lungs swishing out in a loud gasp. She'd never had a man kiss her hand before.

The old foreman at the factory was always trying to catch her unaware and sneak a kiss, and she'd quickly learned to dart away from him and his wayward hands. The old leach was married too.

"Nice to meet you," she said. "I've been looking so forward to this day. Did your mother come with you?"

He shook his head. "No, I didn't tell her about your arrival."

"Oh, why not?"

He glanced at his friend frowning, his brows drawn together, not responding.

"She's not very mobile," Frank replied for her husband.

"I'm so sorry," Katie said wondering about his mother. "She won't be attending our wedding?" she frowned at him. "I can't go to your home without us being married."

She didn't want to make a scene, but the girls had all agreed they wouldn't step into the men's homes without a marriage license in hand. It could ruin their reputations and the man wasn't getting the milk for free.

"No," Daniel said his body rigid. "There's not going to be…"

He gazed at her, hesitating for a long time, mouth open like he wanted to say something, but couldn't.

"Time," he finally responded. A smile graced his dark face, his blue eyes warming as he nodded. "We don't have time to ride out and pick her up and come back to town.

"I thought we would take care of the wedding, if you're ready, right after lunch. You must be famished from your train ride."

Frank glanced at Daniel and smiled.

Her pulse raced at the way he was gazing at her and joy filled her. Sure, her knees were knocking, but everything was falling into place. And her new husband to be was quite dashing. He took her carpet bag from her hand and offered her his arm and her heart leapt in her breast

"Let's get you fed, then we'll go to the courthouse and get married, Miss Maverick," he said, gazing down at her.

Warmth and excitement overwhelmed her. Yes, she was definitely blessed to be marrying such a gentleman.

"Afterwards, I have a bottle of champagne chilling at my office right across the street. We can celebrate your wedding day with a glass of the bubbly before you head to your new home," Frank said grinning at them.

"Thank you. That will help make the day special," Katie said nervous at the thought of marrying this stranger, yet knowing this is why she'd answered the ad.

"I can't wait to meet your mother," she said, wanting to get lost in his gaze. No man had ever had her feeling this way. No one.

"Oh, I'm sure she will feel the same," he said, glancing at his business partner who promptly turned his back. A dart of uneasiness flittered through Katie, but she was not going to let that niggle of doubt ruin her wedding day. She was about to become a bride.

She smiled brightly at him. Her mother had always said that a smile helps any situation and she tried to remember those loving words. "Shall we?"

Chapter Two

Daniel stared at the beautiful young woman, sitting beside him in the buggy, who had become his wife. They'd said their I do's in front of Frank and a witness they'd pulled into the room. It was completely unlike the big society wedding he had with Eloise and yet it felt real.

Walking to the train station earlier, he'd been intent on Frank telling her it was all a big misunderstanding and that Daniel had not sent for her. He'd even made Frank purchase a return ticket on the next train.

But then he'd seen Katie standing on that platform and while part of him knew it was wrong, the lonely man inside him was drawn to the smile on her face, the happiness that radiated from her. She needed a husband and he needed a breath of sunshine to come into his dreary world.

He resisted for all of five minutes before he thought what the hell. He deserved a chance at happiness.

No, it wasn't fair, given she had no idea about the suspicions clinging to him, but he'd been drawn to her the moment he saw her and unable to fight the despair alone any longer. It was selfish and he knew it, but one look at Katie and he'd felt hope for the first time in a year.

He'd been hard since she stepped off the train and he'd learned she was the mail-order bride Frank had ordered. And now he couldn't stop gazing at how lovely his new wife was with her big green eyes, full sweet, tempting mouth and hair that seemed to go on forever. What had he done to get so lucky? Why hadn't some man snatched her up before now?

"Why did you become a mail-order bride," he asked curious as to what would drive a woman to give herself away to a man. "You're beautiful. Weren't there any young men in Lawrenceville?"

She smiled at him coyly. "Thank you. And yes, there are plenty of young men in town, but none were interested in me. I was a factory girl, until the plant was torched by the owner."

"Wow. That's not right. But what about your family?"

She sighed. "In 1880, when I was ten, my family died in a yellow fever epidemic. Somehow I was spared. I was sent to live at the orphanage. The only people I have in the world are my two best friends Genny and Julia and now you," she said with a smile brighter than the noonday sun.

For some reason every time she smiled, his chest warmed and his groin tightened. He'd never had such a physical reaction to a woman before. And if she was as cheerful and warm as she appeared, he couldn't believe his good fortune, but what if it was all a big front? What if she were like Eloise?

"I'm so sorry to hear you lost your loved ones. That's tough."

"I feel fortunate to be alive."

For a moment, he felt guilty about marrying her and expecting her to take care of his mother and his house. But then he realized, he'd probably helped her escape a really bad situation.

Funny, he had intended to meet her at train with no intention of marrying her, but when she'd stepped onto the platform and turned her smiling face towards the sun, he'd been enamored of her beauty, her grace and that smile. It went clear to his toes and back.

He'd kissed her politely on the lips at the wedding ceremony, but he couldn't wait to get her home, get his mother situated, and the two them could escape behind the door to their bedroom. He wondered if she was ready to become his wife in every sense of the word. And would she be a virgin?

"Tell me about your vineyard. I've never known anyone who made wine before."

"Do you like wine?" he asked.

She tilted her head in a way he already adored. "I don't know. The only wine I've had is church wine."

There was such an innocence about her that he hadn't been prepared for. Her clothes were clean and nice, but they were not the latest fashion. She just seemed to have a glow about her and a zest for life that Eloise had never shown. For a woman who life had not showered with advantage, she seemed unaware she was not rich. She seemed genuinely happy and grateful.

"Well, tonight we'll open a bottle from the vineyard and you'll have your first sip of what I hope will someday make our vineyard well known," he said, and also get them out of debt. If not, he could soon be searching for a new occupation and place to live. At least his new wife wasn't accustomed to riches, therefore, she wouldn't miss what they didn't have.

She shivered and immediately he realized he hadn't put the blankets in the buggy before he left, since he'd planned on returning before the sun set.

"Are you cold?" he asked, thinking he wouldn't mind if she sat closer to him. Katie was a delightful young woman and he felt so fortunate to marry her.

Her green eyes gazed at him twinkling like a star in the night sky. "Actually, I'm very nervous about meeting your mother. It's been an exciting day."

Thinking that now was as good a time as any to scoot next to her, he moved until their hips were touching. "My mother can be challenging. She's ill and she has a tendency to take out her frustrations on those around her."

"Oh, I'm so sorry."

"Yes, for six months she's spent more and more time in her chair. I hate to see her health declining," he said softly the sound of the horse trotting on the road crisp in the cold night air.

His mother had never been gentle. She'd always been a woman with a sharp tongue who was quick to wield it.

"Well, we'll just have to see if there is some way to cheer her up and get her moving again," Katie said with determination.

For a moment, he wanted to shield the young woman from the vitriol his mother could spew. He'd been a witness to it, since the day his father died and she'd dried up faster than a spring during a drought. "You don't understand. She's difficult."

Even in the darkness, he could see her turn and raise her brows at him. "You don't think I've handled difficult people before, working in a factory? Living in an orphanage? Working with the Sisters?"

He chuckled. This woman seemed too good to be true. There must be something in her past, something that had kept another man from marrying her.

"You're Catholic?"

"Yes," she said. "What religion are you?"

He gave a short laugh. "Catholic."

"We share the same religion, that's wonderful. I can't wait to get involved in the church and meet your friends," she said smiling at him. "I'm just so happy to be your wife."

He stared at her. Eloise had said those same words to him only a week before they were wed. She couldn't wait to be his wife and was so happy. And the wounds from that marriage had yet to heal. Would Katie hurt him the same way?

Turning the buggy down the road to his home, he knew she was about to face the reality of his situation.

~

As they rode down the lane, Katie stared at the house. The grandeur of the old place filled her with awe. There was so much potential in the home and yet it needed loving care. A shutter hung haphazardly, the paint was peeling and there were no lights shining from the windows. In fact, it appeared dark.

"This is it," Daniel said as he pulled the buggy to a stop in front of the home. "The house needs some work."

"But it has great potential," Katie said gazing at the two-story building. "I can't wait to see what it looks like inside."

Compared to the dingy apartment she'd lived in, this was a mansion. A place where she could make the house into a home, where someday her children would play.

He chuckled. "You're going to be disappointed. That needs work as well. When I bought the place, no one had lived in the house for quite some time. I just haven't had the time or money to put into fixing the inside, yet."

She nodded. "Well, now you have a wife. I can take on some of those jobs."

And at this moment, she wanted to be the best possible partner for Daniel. She didn't want to ever do anything that would make him regret marrying her.

Even in the darkness, she could see there was so much work that needed to be done around the house, but she had never been afraid of work and this was her home. This big, old house where she would birth her babies, and watch them grow until her time on this earth was done.

A sense of purpose and belonging overcame her and she couldn't wait to get inside. She couldn't wait to start on creating her family.

Daniel jumped down from the buggy and then turned back to help Katie alight.

"Why is the house dark?"

"I don't know. I guess mother didn't light the lamps."

Taking her by the hand, they walked to the entrance and he opened the door. He started inside and she pulled him back. He glanced at her. "What?"

She sneaked a curious look in and then gazed at her new husband. "It's good luck to carry your bride across the threshold."

All she could think about was how it would feel to be in his arms, so close, body against body.

She held up her hands. Shaking his head, he reached down and scooped her up cradling her against him. The feel of his arms beneath her buttocks and being so close to him had her breath catching in her throat.

"Oh my."

Her heart was racing like a runaway steam engine and warmth was filling every nook and cranny in her body. Tonight was her wedding night and she thought her lungs were going to stop breathing.

Licking her lips, she gazed up at her husband and wrapped her arms around his neck.

"Welcome home," he said, staring down at her as he carried her across the threshold into the house.

Being in his arms felt heavenly and she was suddenly looking forward to tonight.

"Daniel," a woman screamed. "Is that you, Daniel? Get in here."

The sound of the woman's crass voice screeching had her stomach tensing. Was that his mother?

His face tightened and he dropped his arm and let her slide down the front of him. She felt his body tense and knew that must be his mother. "Coming, Mother."

Taking her by the hand, he glanced at her, his eyes sympathetic as he led her to the back of the house. As they walked into a bedroom large enough to have a sitting area, Katie got her first look at his mother sitting in a wooden wheelchair, staring out the darkened window with no gas lamp burning in the room.

The gray haired elderly woman didn't look frail, but almost maniacal with her face tightly drawn. Now Katie could see why he was warning her. The woman would be daunting to help.

"Where have you been? I've been waiting for you all afternoon. I've been worried sick," the gray-haired dried-up woman demanded. "The ser—"

Katie felt her stomach tighten at the demanding way the woman was talking to her husband. He walked around her chair and lit the gas lamp.

Suddenly she saw Katie, her eyes narrowed and she glared at the girl. "Who is this?"

"Mother, I'd like for you to meet my wife, Katie Maverick O'Malley. Katie, my mother Betty O'Malley."

The old woman's mouth dropped open. "Married. Who is she? And where did she come from?"

Swallowing the fear that threatened to consume her, Katie stepped up and tried to shake the old lady's hand, but she wrenched it away. She could see why her husband had tried to warn her. This would be challenging. "I'm from Lawrenceville, Massachusetts."

Gasping she stared. "You married this girl. How did you meet her? You have terrible taste in women. Why didn't you introduce us before you were married? Are you expecting, girl?"

"Oh," Katie couldn't help the exclamation that flew from her opened mouth. How could she even think she was pregnant. They'd just married.

"Mother!" Daniel cried.

"I'm a mail-order bride," Katie said quietly. "I answered your son's ad in the Grooms' Gazette."

The woman took a deep breath and clutched her chest. "Oh...oh, my medicine, my medicine," she gasped. "The scandal. You're bringing more scandal on us. What were you thinking?"

Daniel grabbed a bottle and a spoon near his mother and poured her dose of the tonic.

"I'm not expecting," Katie said, stunned at her reaction.

Why did his mother think this was scandalous? What had they done that was so wrong? They were married. She'd insisted before she would even come to his house.

All her life she'd fought poverty, doing everything right and yet because she worked in the factory, men thought she was easy and now her husband's mother thought she was a loose woman.

Placing her hands on her hips, she stared at the gray-haired lady whose heart obviously no longer knew love. "Your son, wanted a bride, and I choose him and he accepted me. I truly hope we can become friends. He specifically asked for help with his mother in his ad and I want to help you however I can. I know this is a shock, but I'm now your daughter and you're my mother."

"Ah," the older woman cried and reached out to Daniel. She made gasping noises and flicked her hands like she wanted Katie to leave.

Daniel turned and frowned. "Maybe you should wait for me in the other room."

The excitement and the joy of meeting his mother seemed to drain from her. "I'll light the lamps," she said walking out of the bedroom.

What had she gotten herself into? He'd been right to caution her about his mother, even now she could hear the older woman ranting at Daniel through the bedroom door. The woman was a tyrant, but Katie had faced tough obstacles before.

Everyone, well almost everyone, she eventually won over with kindness. And if anyone needed a gentle touch and a nice word, it was this woman. Her work was certainly cut out for her, but she could do this.

~

Katie walked into the main room and fumbled around until she found a lamp. Quickly she turned it on and a warm glow filled the room. When they arrived, she hadn't been able to see much of the room in the darkness, but it was filled with worn furniture and old rugs that needed cleaning.

The house had a great structure, but needed a woman's touch to make it into a home. She dreamed of this. In fact, she couldn't wait to get started.

Strolling through the house, she lit lamps until the house was filled with light. The kitchen was in much the same disarray. It needed a thorough cleaning. Warmth filled her and she even felt excited about turning this house into a home.

Daniel hurried out of his mother's bedroom and came toward her. "I'm sorry. But you see why I said it could be a challenge."

She reached out and touched his arm. "It's okay. I understand. I've faced tougher battles."

Adjusting to life in the orphanage taught her how to adapt and change. But through it all, her mother's voice was with her, reminding her to smile. She knew she would have to become accustomed to her husband's way of life, but she would not lose her values or her sense of humor.

"I see you lit the lamps."

"Yes, the house is beautiful."

He glanced at her like she was crazy and she realized he had no idea what and where she had lived before. Working in the factory she'd made barely enough to survive.

"I'm glad you like it."

"The layout of the house was well thought out."

Nodding, he took her by the hand and together they walked into the kitchen. "I need a glass of wine."

When he opened a door, she saw there was a staircase. She followed him into a cold basement. Racks with barrels of what she assumed was wine lined the walls. There were shelves of labeled glass bottles. Daniel choose one and turned to her.

"The barrels are this year's crop of grapes. Soon I'll be doing a second racking on the wine. After one more racking, the wine will be ready for bottling and corking."

She didn't understand what he was saying, but soon, very soon she would know more about how to grow and harvest grapes. This was a new adventure.

"I would love for you to show me the vineyards and explain to me how it works."

"One day we'll spend time in the vineyard so you can see," he said seeming closed off once again. Taking her by the hand, he led her up the stairs.

"Is that carpetbag all you brought with you?"

She laughed. What did the man think, she had a trunk full of clothes? A factory worker didn't make enough for fancy dresses. Most of her clothes she'd purchased at a secondhand shop. Her blue silk chiffon, she'd made herself, but even that could be expensive with the cost of fabric.

"A girl like me doesn't have much," she said, not for sympathy but so he would realize she had very little. She didn't need much. And gazing around the house, she had more than she ever dreamed was possible.

"Tomorrow, we'll make space for you in the armoire," he said as he dropped her hand, picked up a bottle opener and two wine glasses. "Let's sit in the parlor."

Following him into the room, she noticed the broadness of his back. He'd worn a dark jacket with a white cotton shirt into town. The color of the jacket brought out the darkness of his hair, which shone in the gas lamplight.

Her husband was more than she'd dreamed of and suddenly she wondered why he'd never married. Soon she would ask him, but not tonight.

While the girls in the orphanage had talked about what to expect on your wedding night, she'd never known what was real and what was fabricated. Sure she'd experienced men trying to have their way with her, on more than one occasion, but she never had a man court her.

And now she was a married woman, about to experience lying with a man for the first time with no prior knowledge of what really happened between a man and a woman.

All she hoped was that she would please her husband. But she didn't know what to expect.

He pointed to the lumpy sofa and she took a seat, her heart beating rapidly. He pried the cork out of the bottle, poured the dark liquid into the glasses and handed one to her, then picked up the other. She'd never seen such fancy drinking glasses and for a moment she stared in awe at the beauty of the glassware.

"To our life together," he said and raised his glass. She lifted hers and he clinked the edge. She'd heard of people toasting, but never participated and she couldn't contain the smile his words filled her with.

She took a sip and thought she was going to spit the horrid liquid out. If this was how wine tasted, why were people so enamored of the drink. Quickly she swallowed and tried to school her features to hide her feelings, but it was too late.

He grinned at her. "I see I don't have to worry about you drinking up all the profits."

"What?" she said confused. "It has an unusual taste."

He laughed. "You'll soon grow to enjoy the flavors. I'll teach you."

"I don't like the taste of coffee either," she said taking another sip. This time the wine warmed her pallet all the way down, spreading heat through her, leaving a luxurious feeling behind. "Oh."

"What's wrong?"

"I feel kind of warm " she said gazing at Daniel. If they had children, she hoped they'd have his beautiful sapphire eyes. "Maybe it was the combination of Frank's champagne and now the wine."

"I think one glass tonight will be quite enough," he said taking the glass from her, his gaze staring at her, making her heart pound like she'd been running down the street.

She was married. Her knees started knocking.

Placing the beautiful crystal on a nearby table, he pulled her against him and his lips covered hers, gently at first and then more pressing. She'd been kissed before, but nothing like her husband was doing. No man had ever ran his tongue over her mouth, sending tingles all over, then slipped in between her lips.

At the convent, they'd taught that girls were to be obedient to their husbands, but the nuns never warned about how it would feel when a man consumed her mouth into his. And then his hand touched her breasts and she pulled back and stared at him, her heart beating rapidly.

"I know we're married," she said breathing heavily, "but I have to tell you, I've never done this before. The nuns only told us we were to submit to our husbands."

Daniel reached out and traced his fingers along her jaw and then rose from the sofa. "Come to bed, Mrs. O'Malley, I think it's time you found out what it's all about."

Katie swallowed, looked at her husband and then took his outstretched hand.

Dear God, she was a married woman about to experience a man for the first time. Part of her couldn't wait and the other part was terrified.

Chapter Three

The next morning, Daniel knew he hadn't given his new wife the kind of wedding night she deserved. He was kicking himself for not taking things slower, but the woman was beyond gorgeous and just one look at her creamy skin and all that long silky hair trailing down her back and he raced like a race horse around the track reaching the goal before she was out of the gate.

And then he listened to her softly crying herself to sleep. What kind of man did that to his wife on their wedding night?

This morning, he would try to make it up to her. Somehow he'd explain that sex between a man and a woman could be beautiful and loving. It was just he hadn't had a woman in a long time, and she was so damn beautiful that he'd forgotten himself. A twelve-year-old boy could have done a better job.

She rolled away from him last night and curled into a little ball, making him feel like he'd been so bad. She recoiled from him.

As the first rays of dawn lit the room, he rolled over and touched her. Her body tensed and he knew she was awake.

"Good morning, Katie," he said softly.

"Good morning," she replied.

Her voice sounded tired.

He sighed. How did he begin this conversation. How did he explain to a virgin that he knew he'd been too quick and rough last night and that if only she'd give him a second chance it could be better.

"About last night," he began.

She jumped out of bed. "Let's not talk about it."

"Give me a chance to explain," he said.

She darted to the washbowl and poured a bowl of fresh water. "No explanation needed. What do you want for breakfast, Mr. O'Malley."

Last night she'd been happy and this morning, she seemed to have thrown up a huge wall, not giving him access. "Normally, I just fix coffee and then go out into the fields. Mother likes toast."

"Do you have eggs?" she asked.

They weren't having an argument, she refused to talk about what had happened last night. At least with a disagreement, he would have a chance to explain or make things right. She wasn't giving him a chance. She only wanted to discuss breakfast.

"Yes," he said. "We have chickens. Martha usually comes over and fixes Mother lunch and also our dinner."

"Fine. I'll fix breakfast and then maybe she can show me around the kitchen. I can cook if I need to."

He watched in fascination as she pulled on her dress. "Katie, I promise you, the next time will be better."

She glared at him in the darkness. "Who said there would be a next time?"

With that, she walked out the door, leaving him to stare at her retreating figure. Cursing beneath his breath, he hauled himself out of bed. They were married. Of course, there would be a next time.

But their situation was different from most married people. They'd met and married on the same day. There had been no courting, no warm-up. And a woman like Katie needed time. He'd do his best to convince her to give him a second chance to show her he could do better, but all he wanted was to pounce on her once again.

He'd been delivered a beautiful woman to become his wife and already he'd made her angry. That didn't take long.

~

Katie reached the kitchen just about the time the first sun rays brightened the room. Quickly she found the coffee pot and beans. Tears prickled her eyelids. What was she crying about?

Sure, she'd dreamed the first time she lay with her husband would be wonderful, but the reality had been it lasted maybe fifteen minutes and most of that time had been him grunting and groaning after he'd rammed into her. Then he'd tried to apologize this morning and she didn't want to hear his excuses.

Her first time should have been special. She didn't know what to expect, but surely lying with a man was more than someone on top of you shoving into your body. If not, she didn't want to experience it again.

He was her husband, and she would bend to his will, but the marital bed was someplace she would avoid as much as possible.

When he walked into the kitchen, she handed him a cup of coffee. "What time will your mother wake up?"

"She'll roll into the kitchen when she's ready. Just fix her some toast and give her either a cup of coffee or tea. That changes with her mood."

After last night, the thought of spending time alone with her mother-in-law was daunting. She had to remember to treat her with kindness and to ignore her nasty comments. Maybe she'd be better this morning since she'd had time to sleep on the fact that her son had married.

"What time will you be back from the vineyard?"

"I'll be back for lunch," he paused and gazed at her. "I promise you it will be better the next time."

Katie wasn't going to give him the pleasure of a response. For years she'd dreamed about what her wedding night would be like and yet last night was nothing like what she'd imagined.

"Mr. O'Malley, I thought I would take a drawer in the armoire and hang my clothes in the wardrobe. I'll also spend some time with your mother today," she said, keeping her back to him.

She didn't want to look at him. She didn't want him to see that last night her childish girlhood dreams of how it would be between her and her husband the first time had been a huge disappointment.

She didn't expect much out of life, since everyone she'd ever loved or cared about had died. She learned early on that you have to absorb the losses, move on, and continue smiling. But whenever she was hurt, it always took time before the voice of reason would have her smiling once again. She needed that time.

He turned her to face him. "Katie, you're so damn beautiful. Men sometimes can't hold back..."

She didn't want to talk about this. No amount of pretty words was going to make her feel any better. "Please, Mr. O'Malley, go to work."

He sighed, reached up and kissed her on the cheek. "I'll see you at lunch."

As he walked out the door, her chest ached. She had so many hopes and dreams and last night they'd come crashing down around her.

She turned back to the coffee and poured herself a cup of the bitter beverage. Sipping on the hot liquid, she gazed around the kitchen that not only needed a good cleaning, but organizing as well.

The sound of wheels thumping, announced the arrival of Mother O'Malley. "Good morning."

The older woman scowled at her. "Why did you marry my son?"

"I needed a husband. Your son had placed an ad in the Grooms' Gazette and I answered the ad."

"See, here is the part of the story I don't believe. My son would never put an ad in a newspaper for a wife. I don't know who you're trying to fool, but my boy would not marry."

"Would you like your toast," Katie asked, not wanting to disagree with the woman and hoping to change the subject. She wasn't going to argue with her.

"Yes," she said sharply.

"Tea or coffee?"

"Coffee."

Katie turned and started the toast for her mother-in-law, contemplating how she could get along with the woman. "Tell me about the house. Did you live here with your husband?"

The woman chuckled, the sound almost evil. "No, my husband's been dead for at least five years. Daniel bought this place not long after he got out of college."

Her husband must have died while Daniel was in college. While it hadn't been that long ago, Katie couldn't help but wonder if his death was what made her so mean-spirited or was she like this before?

"I'm impressed."

"If you married him because he has money, you are in for the shock of your young life. He's broke."

Katie was a little surprised at this announcement. From what she could see it appeared that Daniel had money, but she knew that looks could be deceiving. The factory had seemed like it was doing well and then suddenly everything went wrong.

"Well, that makes two of us. I'm broke as well," she said, trying not to make it sound as mean as she meant it to be, but life had not been easy for her either.

The old woman laughed. "He's about to lose the vineyard. You're going to be back on the street in no time." She gave her an evil smile. "I hope for your sake, that you treat my son with more respect than his first wife. That didn't work out well for her."

Fear spiraled through Katie, gripping her as an icy chill spiraled down her spine. First wife?

~

Daniel never mentioned another wife. He'd never called himself a widower. She swallowed the fear that rose inside her like a volcano, threatening to overwhelm her. Should she be afraid of her new husband? He'd seemed so kind until last night.

"I'm going upstairs to clean," she told her new mother-in-law, knowing she needed time to think without her negative influence.

"Don't change anything," his mother said.

"Why not," Katie asked. From the looks of their bedroom there was so much she could do to make it better. "The house could use a thorough cleaning and straightening," she said, raising her brows at the older woman. "Our home should shine for when we have guests."

The old woman cackled. "Guests? We don't have guests, unless you think the sheriff is a visitor."

A sense of uneasiness tightened her stomach, but Katie tilted her chin. "Any time he stops by, yes, he's a visitor. Now, if you'll excuse me, I want to get started."

Katie hurried from the room, wanting to escape the bitterness oozing from the old woman.

Walking into their bedroom, she saw her virgin blood stained the sheets. Quickly, she stripped them from the bed and poured cold water on the spot, scrubbing at it until she feared she'd rub a hole in the cotton. Tears filled her eyes and her chest ached with disappointment. She'd had such dreams and yet none of them had come true.

Why did it seem her life had been one difficult situation after another. She was due some good fortune, and receiving Daniel's letter and the subsequent wedding, she'd thought her luck was changing, but now she wondered.

What had she gotten herself into? A husband who rutted her like a brood mare and now she learned he was about to lose his vineyard. But the worst revelation, he'd been married before.

Maybe the old woman was crazy. She hoped so.

What did she mean that didn't end well for her? Was she warning Katie to be wary of her own son?

Taking the sheets outside, she finished hanging them in the cold sunshine to dry. Her mother's voice filled her head instilling her with strength.

Work keeps the hands busy and the mind occupied.

Maybe she should just wait and talk to Daniel tonight when he came home. Taking a duster, she went into the bedroom she shared with her new husband.

She gave the room a thorough dusting, beating the curtains, sweeping the wooden floors and wiping down all the furniture. Picking up clothes, she rearranged the room to give more space. While her changes were small, at least she felt the room was cleaner and organized.

Opening the armoire, she folded his undergarments, handkerchiefs and socks, lining them into two drawers for him and two for her. In the bottom of his underwear drawer, she found a folded piece of paper. Opening the parchment paper, she read the document.

Death Certificate for Eloise O'Malley. Died, January 4, 1889. Cause of death – Exposure to Cold.

Fear rose and bubbled inside her chest. She swallowed as she stared at the paperwork. His first wife had been dead more than a year. Exposure to cold. What did that mean?

Was she somehow locked outside or did she become lost? What had caused the death of Eloise O'Malley?

Staring at the death certificate, she hurriedly folded the document and slid it under his underwear, hoping he wouldn't realize she'd seen it.

With a sigh, she hurried down to fix him his lunch. Should she ask Daniel about his wife or should she wait until he told her the truth. Surely, he knew he had to tell her soon because someone other than his mother would let her know about his first wife.

~

When Daniel came home that evening, he was surprised to see his wife had given their cook the night off. He'd gotten busy in the fields and missed lunch completely, even though he'd promised her he would come in.

"Where's Martha?"

"Her grandson is ill, so I sent her home. Dinner is almost ready. Go wash up and then we'll eat."

Walking into the bedroom, he noticed the way the furniture sparkled, the bed was made and even his dresser was cleaned off. The curtains were open to let in the setting sun and the room seemed brighter and cleaner. His wife had made progress today on his home and while that pleased him, he knew there was still much to do.

Eloisa had hated housework and told him to hire servants. The only servant they had in the house was Martha, the woman who cooked and also helped with his mother, giving her a bath. But today, Katie was cooking and from the smell of the meal, he couldn't wait to eat.

Pulling open the drawer, he realized she'd done what he told her and moved things around. Now his underwear were all folded nice and tidy, his socks and handkerchiefs were in order and – fear ripped through him. Hurriedly he searched to find the document he'd hidden. Eloisa's death certificate.

The parchment paper lay folded in the same drawer where it had been hidden. But had she opened and read the document? Had she learned he'd been married once before?

He should have told her last night, but he hadn't wanted to ruin the evening by talking about the past. Even now he just wanted to make up to his wife and get a second chance at making her happy. To show her that sex between them could be better than what she'd experienced last night. He'd made a huge mistake, letting his body take over and not taking his time.

Frankly, he'd been surprised she'd been a virgin. A woman who'd worked in a factory, lived on her own and had to take care of herself. Maybe he was being foolish, but he'd not expected her to be an innocent.

When he entered the dining room, his mother gazed at him from her chair at the table. "How is work in the fields?"

"Good. We're prepping the soil for the next season. Plus we're still straining the last batch of wine we produced. What about you, Mother, what did you do today?"

She laughed the sound almost vicious. "I broke in your new wife."

There were times he hated his mother. Since her injury, she'd become a cruel old woman. The mother he remembered had disappeared and he wished something would bring her back. "I'm sure Katie was very helpful to you, Mother."

"You can't lie to her anymore. She knows."

"I haven't lied, Mother."

"But you didn't tell her everything did you?"

Why did she make it sound so evil? A man didn't want to tell his bride about his first wife on their wedding night.

It didn't seem right. And he hadn't been the one to send her that letter.

"Thank you for divulging that information for me. I had planned on telling her when the time was right. I didn't think that was appropriate talk the first night of our marriage," he said sarcastically, wishing his mother would learn to keep her mouth shut.

The older woman cackled and he wondered like he often did of late, if she was losing her mind. Could illness destroy not only a body, but a mind as well?

"You'll pay for your sins," she said softly. "I know what you did."

"What do you think I did?" he asked. She thought he'd killed Eloise.

"I saw Eloise leave that night."

He sighed and closed his eyes, wishing things were easier. She'd told him before that she saw his wife run out into the snow. But why?

The door to the kitchen opened and Katie carried a big pot to the table where she sat it down. "I just need to bring in the serving utensils. Mother O'Malley do you want anything besides water to drink?"

"I'm fine."

Katie walked out.

"She's calling you Mother O'Malley. That has to be a good sign."

His mother glanced at him her brown eyes darkening. "No. Not really. It just means she's polite."

"And polite isn't good?"

She shrugged. "It won't win me over."

Shaking his head, he laughed. "I've been your son for almost thirty years and that hasn't won you over. I hardly expect her being here one day is going to give her any advantage."

Once his mother had been a controlling woman, but now she was hateful and bitter and often times there was nothing nice about her. Yet, she was his mother and he prayed for the return of the mother he use to know.

"You're being impertinent."

"Truthful, Mother, truthful. There's a difference. What happened to make you so angry?"

"You know what happened—"

"An accident. You've let a carriage accident turn you into an embittered old woman," he said being frank. He was tired of her vile tongue and wanted peace in his house for a change.

"And whose fault—"

His mother stopped in mid-sentence when Katie walked in carrying utensils. She glanced between the two of them. "Am I interrupting?"

What could he say, the same argument he'd had for the last five years with his mother? Over whose fault the carriage accident was? Yes, it'd been his father's fault, but he was dead. It had cost him his life. But what could they change? It was too late and he just wished his mother would accept the accident and get on with her life in a happy way.

"No," he said glancing at Katie. "We're waiting on you."

She sat at the table, placing the spoons in the dishes. Waiting she glanced at him as he picked up his utensils.

Clearing her throat she said, "Grace? Do you not say grace at a meal?"

His mother laughed and looked at her son. "You are in so much trouble."

"Of course," he said, and bowed his head as he said the blessing.

Since the death of his father in a carriage accident and then with Eloise passing so mysteriously, he had all the trouble he could manage. Grieving his father, trying to help his mother and then his wife died. He was young. He wanted his life to be happy, not surrounded by grief and mystery. And Katie's bright smile was like a beacon in a stormy sea.

Later that evening after all his attempts to try to smooth over the hurt with his new wife, he noticed she quietly slipped up the stairs for bed.

He gave her about five minutes before he hurried up to their bedroom eager to right the bad start to their marriage.

When he walked in, she was standing in her nightgown, washing her face.

"I like the changes you made. The bedroom looks nice, thank you," he said quietly as he slipped off his pants and shirt. He wanted to already be in bed waiting on her when she crawled in. Then he would pull her into his arms and show her how great sex between a man and woman could be.

Slipping beneath the covers, he was shocked when he felt a rolled up blanket dividing the bed.

"What the hell?" he questioned, raising the coverlet.

He almost laughed out loud. Did she really believe that a rolled up blanket was going to keep him from her? The urge to yank it up and throw it across the room was strong, but he took a deep breath and released it slowly. Wouldn't it be better to respect her wishes with the hope that soon, he could woo her back into his arms?

"It's a bedroll. To remind you to stay on your side of the bed and I'll sleep on mine," she said crawling under the coverlet beside him.

"Katie, we're married. I know I was in too big a hurry last night, but it will be better."

Somehow he had to convince her to let him try again and this time, he'd better make certain it was good for her or this could become a serious problem in their marriage.

"You don't get a second chance at a wedding night. I need some time to recover from the first one," she said and slipped over on her side, giving him her back.

With a sigh, he rolled over. Women had such grandiose dreams of the first time and for a man, it was still just sex. There was no one to blame, but himself. If he hadn't been in such a hurry, tonight would be different. He would be having sex every night instead of just once. He'd disappointed her and he didn't like that feeling.

Already he was learning that his sweet, bubbly wife had a strong will that could twist a man's insides into a knot. He wanted her in the worst way and she was having nothing to do with him.

"If you weren't so damn beautiful, this wouldn't have been a problem," he said in the darkness and knew the moment the words slipped out of his mouth, it was the wrong thing to say.

"Oh, I should have been ugly, then you would have taken my virginity thinking of how you didn't want to hurt me? I don't think so. Go to sleep Mr. O'Malley. But in the morning, I expect to be told about your first wife."

He cursed. She knew. She'd read the death certificate in his drawer and knew.

Chapter Four

The next morning when Katie awoke, her husband had already gone to the fields. That was certainly one way to get out of a conversation. Avoid your wife. But he'd have to come back for lunch, if not dinner and when he came home, he would not escape the story about his wife this time. It wasn't that she was afraid of Daniel, but why hadn't he been upfront about his first wife? All he had to do was say how she passed away.

Sure, now that she'd read the death certificate, she was curious, but all it took was one conversation.

After she'd straightened up the bedroom, she hurried downstairs to the kitchen. It was then she heard the tinkling of Mother O'Malley's dinner bell.

She hurried to her bedroom door. "Good morning, Mother O'Malley," she said yanking back the curtains.

"Where have you been?" the old woman asked from her bed. "I'm weak this morning and can't seem to reach my chair."

Katie was determined not to let the old biddy get to her today. She was going to shower this woman with so much kindness that she would drown in the happiness Katie bestowed upon her.

"I've been upstairs straightening. I'm sorry, I didn't hear your bell," she said walking to the woman and helping her out of bed. "I thought Martha was here. Do you need help dressing."

"No, Martha, will help me with that. Shut those blinds. It's too bright in here," she said with a sneer.

"Sunshine brightens the soul and clears fog from the brain," Katie said trying to be positive and uplifting, yet feeling like she was dragging a reluctant soldier.

Inside this woman, there had to be some goodness. She was, after all, Daniel's mother and her son was a good man.

How could he turn out so well if his mother had always been like this? No, something must have changed her.

"I don't suffer from cloudy thinking or need my soul brightened. Go fix me some tea. I'll be in the kitchen in a moment," she said scowling at Katie.

With a sigh Katie left the room. "Patience, Lord give me patience."

When she arrived in the kitchen, Martha was there and had already started the tea. "Good morning, Mrs. O'Malley."

The sound of someone calling her by her married name startled and thrilled her. It would take some getting used to, but she liked the way it sounded.

"Good morning. Oh, you heard her."

The older black woman chuckled. "Couldn't miss the sound of her bell. Sounds like she's not feeling well. When she gets in this kind of mood, you can't make her happy."

Katie shook her head. "Has she always been this way?"

"Since the carriage accident that killed her husband and injured her. She's never fully recovered is what I've been told. I've only been here as long as Mr. O'Malley owned the land."

"That's sad. How long ago was that?"

Maybe this was what had changed her into the person she was now. Didn't all of life's events alter us in small ways, but deaths and births, those were branded onto us and shaped us more than most things in life.

"At least over five years," the colored woman said as she prepared her toast.

"Okay, I know the accident was traumatic and sad and left her injured, but no one should be allowed to wallow in misery for five years."

What if the death of her parents and siblings had left her bitter and angry? What would she be like today? And she had been angry. She'd lost everything she'd known and forced to move into the orphanage.

"They were going to visit Mr. O'Malley at college, when the wheel busted on their carriage sending it over on its side. Her husband, Mr. O'Malley, hit his head on a rock and died instantly. Mrs. O'Malley, injured her back. Now she can only walk a short distance before needing her chair. Between you and me, I think she could do better if she wanted to. But this way she gets all the attention."

Until that moment, Katie had felt sorry for the cranky, older woman, but she firmly believed a person had no right to be a whiner or a complainer and make others miserable. She had to find a way to help her understand.

"Thanks, for telling me, Martha. I'm going to think on what we can do to change this situation. Because I'm not going to let her bully me."

The woman shrugged. "I need to know if I accept my work from you or Mrs. O'Malley?"

"The only change is that I will give you orders on meals and the housekeeping, which we will get started on once you've got her settled."

The older woman frowned. "I didn't take any orders from the first Mrs. O'Malley. In fact she didn't do much with the house."

"Well, I can tell you that's going to change. I'll be handling all the household duties, the menus and the cleaning schedule. We're going to make this house look radiant once again."

The older woman's brows raised. "I'll talk to Mrs. O'Malley and make certain that's okay with her, since I'm her servant."

"Do that and I'll take to Mr. O'Malley about hiring us more hands," Katie said not really understanding why the elderly servant was not following her lead.

Taking a deep breath she decided to see what the woman thought of Eloise, hoping she would give her some insight into how the house was run.

"So Eloise didn't run the household?"

"No, ma'am."

"Did she do the menus, the cleaning? What did she do around here?"

The cook's face suddenly blanched and she shifted away from Katie and finished fixing the tray to take into Mother O'Malley's room. "I didn't have much to do with the first Mrs. O'Malley."

The woman's demeanor changed and she was no longer as friendly as before. In fact she'd become almost cold and Katie knew that no matter what she asked, she wasn't going to say. With the mention of Eloise, the cook had gone from talking freely to being reserved and tight-lipped. What was so secret about Eloise O'Malley's death?

"I better get this tray into her room."

"Is your grandson better?" Katie asked wanting to delay her departure so she could think of more questions to ask her.

"Yes, he's feeling much better."

"Good, I need some help around the house. Would he be interested in dusting in high places?"

There was so much to be done around here and some things she needed someone who could crawl on ladders. She was getting rid of the dust, but could she wipe out the past as well?

"I'll have him come up here after lunch," she said picking up the tray and walking towards the door.

"Great! We're going to clean this house thoroughly. When Daniel comes home, he's going to be shocked."

"I hope so, Mrs. O'Malley."

Katie watched the colored woman leave the room. Why did she feel like the old house held secrets.

~

Later that afternoon, Katie was finishing the cleaning and rearranging of the front parlor, when she heard a buggy drive up in the front circular driveway. She had spent the afternoon with the help of Thomas, Martha's grandson beating the rugs and drapes, moving furniture, polishing the wood until it gleamed, scrubbing the hardwood floors and putting down a nice shine with new wax. They were just moving the sofa back when the knock sounded on the door.

The kid was in his teens and when she'd offered to pay him for his time, he'd been more than willing to assist her all afternoon.

Glancing out the window, she saw Frank and opened the door. "Good afternoon, Frank."

He reached down and pecked her on the cheek. "I had to come by and see how my favorite newlyweds are doing?"

"Please come in," she said, and moved to let him enter the parlor.

Being called a newlywed felt strange. Yes, they were married, but it had only been days and there were still so many unresolved issues between them. Did all newly married couples have these problems or had she gotten herself into a fine mess?

Frank glanced around and nodded approvingly. "You're making this house look like a home again. Great job."

"Thomas, please get Mr. O'Malley from the fields," she said, to the young boy who had been helping her.

Martha and Betty were here with her, but she'd feel better if Daniel. This was after all his friend.

"Sorry, I'm not dressed more presentable, but we've spent the afternoon cleaning. I'm going room by room through our home making it shine," she said, pulling her head scarf off, letting her hair fall loose past her shoulders.

Frank's eyes widened. "You've done a remarkable job so far. I can't wait to see what it looks like when you're finished."

"It'll take time," she replied, pleased with today's progress.

A bell clanging furiously from the back of the house, resounded in the parlor.

"Please have a seat. I've sent for Daniel, but let me see what Mother O'Malley needs," she said, walking towards her room.

The old woman must have heard the door knocker and wondered who was here. Well, she wasn't going to tell her. She would just have to join them if she wanted to know. It was time she reentered society, but as a happier person.

Walking into the darkened room, she glanced at her mother-in-law sitting in her chair staring gloomily at nothing. "Where have you been? I'd like for you to read to me for a while."

"I can't, we have a guest," Katie said. "I think you should join us."

The woman's eyes narrowed. "If it's Frank Lowe, absolutely not. That boy is using my son, just like you."

The words were harsh. And she wanted to respond but decided no, that's what Betty wanted. Katie turned to leave.

"What, you're not going to deny it?"

She glanced back at the woman. "Why should I? You're going to believe what you want. And if Frank is using Daniel, why aren't you out there trying to learn more from him so you can protect your son."

"Excuse me. Can't you see I'm in a wheelchair."

Somehow Katie thought this must be an excuse she used often and she wasn't going to let her incite sympathy.

"Yes, but that doesn't make you invisible or not useful. I'd be happy to wheel you into the parlor if you'd like to join us. You're still Daniel's mother and a loving person. Come join the conversation."

"No. And you shouldn't be talking to him either. You're a married woman with no chaperone in the house."

This was why she'd sent for Daniel. She feared that his mother would start insinuating lies and she had to protect herself.

"You're here and I sent young Thomas to the fields for Daniel."

"What can I do? I can't protect you."

The woman had more excuses and complaints. "All you have to do is let me roll you into the parlor and be with us until Daniel arrives and then you're free to leave."

"Hrrmph. Why should I worry about your reputation. You won't be here long," she said smiling in a way that was just mean.

Katie forced a smile on her lips. "For too long, people in this house have walked around you carefully giving you too much power. I expect more from you. You are the matriarch of the family and should lead by example. If you want to be around your future grandchildren, then I expect you to be a nice person. I won't put up with you treating me or anyone I care about badly, including your son."

"I'm not changing for you or anyone else," she hissed. "You'll be leaving soon. The first woman my son married, didn't stay and neither will you."

Fury rolled through Katie at the mention of Eloise. Until that moment, she had been trying to make the old witch realize she was pushing people away, but now she was just mad at how she was trying to instill fear in her and that wasn't right.

"Excuse me, we have guests and I'm not going to stay here and argue with you. If you want to join us, please do, but try to wear a smile. I know you've forgotten what that is, but I'll not put up with you being disrespectful to our guests."

Katie turned and walked out of the room, running smack into Daniel's big solid chest.

She gazed into her husband's dark blue eyes. Wrapping his arms around her, he kept her from falling. Why did the man's body feel so good against her own? She licked her lips as she stared up at him.

"Is Mother giving you trouble," he asked.

"Nothing, I can't handle," she said, wondering if he would back her or his mother and not wanting to find out.

"Frank, is here," she whispered.

"Frank, can wait," he said as his lips covered hers.

For a moment all the secrets between them disappeared. The hurt and anger from their wedding night vanished as his mouth covered hers in a kiss that felt like he wanted to consume her. And she wanted to let him. Whatever magic his mouth possessed, it swept through her and she felt herself turn to almost liquid in his arms.

He smelled of the earth and the fields with a hint of the distillery and she quickly realized she liked her husband's manly scent. Tilting her head, he slowly released her mouth, his breathing quick and shallow.

"That, Mrs. O'Malley, is the proper way a man should kiss his wife hello."

She licked her lips. "Not bad, Mr. O'Malley, much better than the other night."

Why was it her body responded to his kisses, his touch, but when they'd come together...it had been bad.

With a laugh he shook his head. "I fear that night is going to haunt me for a long time."

"A girl dreams of her wedding night," she said softly. "And mine was disappointing."

"What can I do to make it up to you?"

What could she say? At least he was trying, but she wasn't willing to try again and she knew that would be his response. Give me a second chance. No, she wasn't ready.

Just then they heard a crash from the parlor.

"I think our guest grows impatient," she said.

Taking a step out of his arms, she hurried to see what Frank had broken, knowing if her husband kissed her much more she could see that bedroll disappearing.

~

Katie was grateful that Martha had cooked more than enough food when Daniel invited Frank to stay and have dinner with them. Sitting around the table, listening to her husband and his friend, she realized Frank knew very little about the vineyard.

"How did you two men meet?" Katie asked passing the brown gravy.

Mother O'Malley made a snorting noise and Katie frowned at the woman. She wanted to learn as much as possible about her husband's business and his partner. Never again, would she depend on things being as they seemed.

The fire that destroyed the factory taught her a valuable lesson. Understand as much as possible about your livelihood or be surprised when things change without warning.

"We went to the same college," Frank said. "Daniel and I belonged to the same fraternity."

"We dated the same girls," Daniel said with a laugh.

Frank grinned. "Until you got caught."

"I didn't know she'd been seeing you," Daniel said with a laugh. "She tricked us both. Then married another classmate."

"I think we were both lucky not to fall for Clara Sue Whittaker. Last I heard, she had five kids and another one on the way," Frank said.

Daniel shrugged and glanced at his wife. "That wouldn't be so bad."

"So once you were out of college, you decided to start a vineyard together?"

They laughed and glanced across the table at one another. "No, the grapes had to extract a toll on me first. It wasn't until I was about to go under that Frank offered to invest in the vineyard. We've been partners going on two years now."

Only two years and Daniel had only been in business four years. Yet they seemed to work together and were good friends. Just like Julia and Ginny.

"Maybe I was crazy for sinking money into a wine operation. Thomas Jefferson couldn't make a go of a vineyard in Virginia and yet Daniel convinced me this is the perfect country for growing. Cold winters, cool springs and wet summers. The perfect location for harvesting grapes and making wine."

"And this year our first bottles will be ready to sell."

For the first time, Daniel would be trying to sell the finished product. Now would be when they learned if the wine was tasty enough for people to buy. Now would decide their future.

Frank leaned back. "I still think the land would be better suited for tobacco farming. The crops are easier to grow, you have a quicker turn around and the profits are instantaneous. And if you didn't want to be a farmer, I have an investor who is willing to offer you top dollar for the land."

Katie raised her eyes from the plate of food to stare at her husband and then Frank. Would Daniel consider selling the land and if he did, where would they go?

She watched her husband's face tighten and even from the short time she'd gotten to know him, she knew that gathering of his forehead and the way his eyes darkened was not a receptive signal. Frank would do well to back off.

"I'm not going to raise tobacco as it depletes the soil. And the only way I'm selling this place is if I go under. It's our first season with actual wine to sell, give the vineyard a chance to earn a profit."

Katie glanced nervously about. Daniel had raised his voice to Frank and she could see he was frustrated with him for even mentioning tobacco farming. The two men were both strong willed and yet Daniel was more determined than Frank to make the vineyard profitable. She could see her husband was truly the one who craved the success.

Frank lifted his wine glass to his lips. "And it's a fine tasty wine. But how many bottles of the vino are you going to have to sell before you make a profit?"

"It's going to take at least two years before we will start to see any profit. I told you this when you agreed to become my partner."

Listening, Katie knew the two men were friends, yet there seemed to be an undercurrent running through the room that left her nervous. She glanced at her mother-in-law and saw she was watching the two men with interest.

"But selling the land could get you instantaneous money. Let me bring the buyers out, the Southern Virginia Tobacco and Land Company to see the farm."

Silence filled the dining room and she could see a vein throbbing in Daniel's neck. Did Frank want out of the partnership? Why was he bringing buyers out to their place. She'd only been his wife for days, but she was with Daniel. She didn't want him to sell the property.

"No," Daniel said his voice rising. "I'm not selling the land."

"Is anyone ready for dessert? Martha made a peach cobbler," Katie said rising from her chair, wanting to divert the men's attention from their explosive conversation to a more desirable topic.

"Yes, please," Frank said.

"Me, too," Daniel acknowledged and his mother nodded.

She went into the kitchen and brought out the cobbler and set it on the table. She cut them each a slice, handing her husband the first piece. He gazed at her and she could see the questions in his eyes and wondered at them. What was he thinking?

His mother gazed at Frank and then her son. "You're right, Frank, tobacco is king around here. One of these days that will come to an end, whereas wine is a relatively new undertaking in Virginia. Sometimes it's better to be different from everyone else."

Katie smiled at her mother-in-law, trying to give her encouragement. For the first time she'd said something intelligent and positive and not full of contempt. Maybe she was learning.

"Yes, Mother, you're right. Though several times, it's been tried and failed. I could fail, but until I do, I'm not giving up."

Frank shrugged. "Then winemakers we are."

Katie noticed the stubborn tilt in Frank's chin and the way his brown eyes flashed when he finally admitted defeat. But had he really conceded or was he just waiting for another opportunity to convince Daniel to give up the vineyard he loved?

~

Daniel escorted Frank into the parlor for a glass of brandy before he left for the evening. Sure, there were times that Frank was more of a nuisance than a helper, but he'd come through financially when Daniel needed help. And when Eloise had died and the town turned against him, Frank had been his only friend. They were as close as brothers and sometimes they disagreed just like siblings.

"It appears this marriage agrees with you. The house has never looked better and your wife, she's delightful. I think ordering you a mail-order bride was a great solution."

What could he say? Katie was a delight and the only problems in their marriage so far were because of him. But there were too many secrets and he didn't know how to tell her the truth.

How did you tell a woman he wasn't the one who ordered her or that his previous wife died suspiciously and he was the person everyone suspected of killing her?

Glancing around, Daniel shook his head. "She doesn't know I wasn't the one who placed that ad. She doesn't know about what happened to Eloise. Mother told her I'd been married before and she found the death certificate."

"How did she find the death certificate?"

People believing that he murdered his wife he couldn't control, but he'd just shoved the document in his drawer and tried to forget its existence. That time in his life was painful and he tried not to think of those dark days.

"While I was out in the fields, she rearranged and cleaned out the armoire. I forgot I just shoved that document in my drawer, never wanting to see it again." He cursed. "It has the cause of death on the document."

The corners of Frank's mouth turned down in a frown and his eyes darkened. His breathing changed and for a moment, Daniel thought he was angry, yet he had stood by his side when everyone else believed the worst about him, including his mother.

"Exposure. Isn't that what the death certificate says?" Frank said, his voice rough. "You've never told me what caused the argument that night. All you've ever said was that you awoke and she was gone."

The reason for Eloise's death, the reason for their argument was something he'd never shared with anyone. And just thinking about that night caused his stomach to clench. "She was leaving me."

He'd told the sheriff he suspected there was someone else, but he'd never mentioned the argument. He feared if he told them they'd fought about her leaving, then the authorities would think he was a killer. And he had not killed his wife.

Frank stood and began to pace the parlor, sipping his brandy even faster. "That's hardly a reason for her to go running out into the cold. It was one of the worst storms of the season. Why would she go out of the house? She wasn't stupid."

No, Eloise was anything but stupid. She was manipulative, conniving and used to getting her own way. She had to have the very best and Daniel had never made her happy. In some ways her death was a relief.

"Why are you asking these questions now? Because I mentioned the death certificate? Or are you having second thoughts since I've remarried?"

Pain clenched Daniel's chest. He'd relived that conversation a thousand times over wondering what had sent her running out into the snow in her nightgown. When she'd gone to sleep in the spare bedroom, he'd been resigned to her leaving the next morning. He had given up trying to make her happy. And yet guilt ate at him and the wondering at her reasoning, why would she go out in the weather, the snow?

"No, I know you didn't kill your wife," Frank said quietly. "I've wondered what would send her racing from the house."

"I went to sleep thinking she was going to leave me, and when I woke, she was gone. At first I thought she'd left already, but then I found her suitcase still in the bedroom. Why would she leave everything behind? The woman loved her things, she would not have gone without them. So I started searching for her."

"She had a lover," his mother's voice came from the doorway and he stared at her in surprise.

Frank turned and smiled at his mother. "Mrs. O'Malley, you do talk. How do you know?"

"I saw them together. She was pregnant."

Pain clenched his chest. He hadn't wanted her to die. They were having problems, but he'd never have wished death on her. But pregnant? That could explain the reason she'd left.

Silence filled the room and Daniel, stared. "Mother, I think you're mistaken."

"I know the changes a woman's body goes through when she's expecting a child. Eloise was expecting."

Daniel thought back to the last time he'd made love to his wife. It had been months before she left. If she was pregnant, the child wasn't his.

Frank glared at his mother. Finally, he cleared his throat. "It's late. I should be going."

Katie walked into the room from the kitchen. She glanced around the room at the three people, obviously sensing the tension. "Are you leaving?"

Staring at his new wife, he felt a rush of hope for a new chance at a good marriage, with children and love and a successful winery. That's all he wanted out of life. The vineyard was a work in progress and now he had to create a loving relationship with his new wife.

"Yes, I need to get back to town. I have clients to meet in the morning," Frank said. "Thank you for such a lovely dinner and a charming evening."

"Any time," Katie said as she walked him towards the door. She took his jacket off the rack and handed it to him. "Please, I know you and Daniel are good friends. Drop in any time."

Daniel watched his friend and then he turned and touched the tip of his hat.

"Good night."

"Good night," Daniel replied.

Tonight Frank had seemed to irritate him more than he'd actually enjoyed his company. First with his talk of selling the land and then with his questions about Eloise, who he had yet to tell Katie about. For the first time since college, he wondered if Frank really was his good friend or simply a man who liked to make business deals.

Daniel, watched as Katie shut the door. "It's getting chilly out there."

He thought of Eloise. Was it true she'd been pregnant? Could his mother be right? And was that the reason she was leaving him? She'd told him there was someone else, but she'd never said anything about a pregnancy.

He walked to Katie, glanced down at his new wife and fear spiraled through him, centering in his chest until he thought it would explode. Would Katie also cheat on him? He couldn't take that chance.

"Do me a favor."

"What?" Katie said, glancing up at him, her impish smile brightening her face. She was a ray of sunshine in his home and already he felt possessive of this woman. She'd moved in and was making over his home and he prayed she would change the atmosphere from gloom and doom to happiness. He so desperately wanted to feel joy again.

And damn, but he wanted to carry her upstairs and slowly erase her memory of their wedding night. This time the night would be so memorable, his wife would never forget.

"Don't let Frank or any man into the house without me being here," he said, knowing his reasons were an overreaction, but not caring. Katie was his wife, and yes, they had a few problems, but he wanted to make this marriage work. And he couldn't take a chance on her cheating.

"Why?" she asked staring up at him in shock. "I didn't do anything wrong. I sat him in the parlor and sent Thomas for you."

"I know," he said. "But something is warning me not to let anyone in the house without me being here. I listen to those premonitions and when I haven't, it's cost me."

Behind him, his mother started to cackle like an old witch. He'd forgotten all about her being in the room.

"He's afraid you're going to cheat on him, just like Eloise. She'll leave you just like Eloise and her fate will be the same."

A chill went through Daniel and he stared at his mother. Good God could she have killed Eloise that night? She knew his wife was cheating, she thought she was pregnant, but how could a woman in a wheelchair force Eloise into the cold?

Chapter Five

All the enjoyment of the evening drained out of Katie. She glanced at his mother and couldn't take the old hag cackling at her husband any longer. "It's time for bed."

"She's going to leave you," his mother called out.

Daniel's face was ashen as she walked out of the parlor. With a heavy heart, Katie pushed his mother down the hallway to her room.

"Why do you have to be so mean? Can't you see you upset him?" Katie asked wanting to roll her into her room and leave her.

"Eloise cheated on him. You'll cheat on him too," she whispered. "People cheat."

"How do you know she cheated on him?"

What if Eloise had been innocent? She wasn't here to defend herself and until Katie had proof, she refused to believe it about the woman she'd never met. Maybe she was naive.

"I saw the two of them."

"Who was she with?"

"It was dark, I couldn't see, but I have my suspicions."

"How do you know it was her?"

She laughed. "You really don't want to believe that Eloise had an affair."

"No, I don't. The woman is dead. I didn't know her and I'm not talking bad about a dead person. And for your information, I will never cheat on my husband."

The thought of Daniel being with another woman, left her heart aching. No, their marriage had its problems, but that could never be solved by being with someone else.

His mother threw up her hands. "That's what everyone says in the beginning, but then temptation lures them away," she whispered. "Temptation is an evil mistress that makes promises she never intends to keep."

"Did you cheat on your husband?"

The older woman swirled around in her chair and pointed her finger at her. "Don't get sassy with me, young miss."

"You didn't answer the question? Did you cheat on your husband? Did your husband have an affair?"

Katie stared at her mother-in-law and saw the answer on her face. She didn't have to tell her yes or no. The pain was in her expression and in her eyes. She didn't know which one had committed adultery, but just seeing the result was enough to convince her, she would never dishonor her marriage.

"Just leave me. I can get into bed by myself," she said.

"If you can get into bed by yourself, then why do you need a chair?"

"I need a chair because my legs don't work?"

Katie felt bad for her mother-in-law, but she also knew it was time to stop her from being so mean and spiteful.

"You know, I feel sorry for you up to a point, but there comes a time, when you're so mean and nasty that I don't care if you need my help. I warn you that I am not letting you berate and mistreat me. Or you could find yourself ringing your bell and no one responding."

"You wouldn't dare. I'll tell my son."

Threats strengthened Katie's resolve to stand up to the woman.

"I'll tell him the truth that while he's gone during the day, you walk alone."

"You hussy," she screeched, her eyes growing large. "Leave."

"Gladly. Rest peacefully," Katie said and walked out the door.

Now all she had left to do was talk to Daniel about his first wife. She wanted to know what happened to the woman. Had she cheated on him? And why did her death certificate list exposure?

Walking back into the parlor, he wasn't there. She hurried up the stairs. She hadn't been gone that long and she wanted this secret between them exposed. It was time he told her the truth.

Opening the bedroom door, she heard his soft even breathing. The man was sound asleep. While she'd been taking care of his mother, he'd gone to bed. This morning he'd avoided her at breakfast and now he was snoring. Yet his kiss had been filled with passion and something more she still didn't understand.

The day had been draining. Her first week here had exhausted her and now she was beginning to doubt why she agreed to marry a man she knew nothing about. Who hadn't told her about his first wife. Who had left out so much about his mother.

And yet she couldn't help but remember how hopeful she'd felt when they pulled up the driveway and she'd seen her new home. It was a mansion compared to the cramped quarters where she'd lived before. And yet, it seem to come with a price. So many secrets.

~

An hour later, unable to sleep, though her body was exhausted her mind still raced. It was a good time to write to her friends to let them know she had safely arrived.

November 10, 1890

Dear Genny and Julia,

Sorry for writing to you both at the same time but it's just easier this way. I wanted to let you know I arrived safely in Charlottesville, Virginia. My husband's vineyard is a small ways from town, so I don't know when you'll receive this letter. We were married the same day I arrived, and I'm now Katie O'Malley. His home is large, but rather run-down and I'm working like crazy to clean the place. It could be so beautiful.

His mother is a poor soul who's suffered much, and takes her misfortune out on everyone around her and most especially me. She's dreadful. The woman uses a wheelchair because she says she can't walk, though I've caught her at least once getting around without the chair. She is mean and vile and no matter how hard I try to be nice, she's ugly to me.

I'll keep trying, though, right now I'm tired. But as my mother use to say a smile can always brighten a situation. I'm smiling as I write this letter to you, hoping things will improve.

My husband has the most beautiful blue eyes and black hair. He's so handsome, but he has secrets. He never mentioned in his letter that he's a widower. Not that it would have made any difference, I just would have liked to have known in advance. And he's not very open about what happened to his first wife. His mother tells me she was cheating on him, but I don't know if that's true. He hasn't told me about her. He's closed off.

There is so much potential here. If he would just open up and trust me, we could make this place into a magnificent home that sold great bottles of wine.

I'm trying not to get discouraged, but tonight, I'm feeling low. At a dinner party, my mother-in-law screamed out that my husband's wife was cheating on him and I'll cheat too. I was mortified. And then the old bitty wanted me to put her to bed. If I wasn't a good Christian woman, I would have smothered her.

The weather in Virginia is cold this time of year, but it's not miserable like in Massachusetts. I'm hoping my next letter will tell you that I'm blissfully happy, expecting my first child, and things couldn't be better. But for now, keep me in your prayers, like I keep you in mine.

Please write and tell me how you are. I hope your situation has been better than mine. I miss you all so much, I can hardly stand it.

Much Love,
Katie

~

The next morning, Daniel expected to leave for town before Katie was up. Opening the cash box, he realized there was money missing. He'd had close to one hundred dollars for household expenses. Money he needed to purchase more wood to build stands for the new barrels that would soon arrive. Katie didn't seem the type to steal, but it concerned him money was missing. Did she even know where the cash box was kept?

Closing the box he tried to determine what to do. He didn't want to ask Frank for more cash, but what little was left in the bank, he really didn't want to take out. Hopefully, he would soon start to see profits coming in. If not, he could be in trouble within six months.

Putting the box back in his desk, he glanced around at the office. It didn't appear to have been cleaned and she'd been busy in every other room in the house.

Stepping out the door, he almost ran smack into Katie.

"Good morning," she said. "I hope you slept well last night."

She was so damn bright and cheery in the mornings. He loved that about her and yet it took some getting used to. "Very well, thanks. What about you?"

He was asking because he knew she wanted to talk about Eloise, but after last night he'd felt drained. She was in the past and he wanted to leave her there and not spend so much time digging up old hurts. First Katie, then Frank and even his mother seemed to hang on to that dreadful situation. Why couldn't they all just think about today and not concentrate on the past.

"Great! I'm fixing eggs for breakfast. How many would you like?"

"None. I need to get on the road."

"Oh, where are you going?"

"I'm going into town to buy lumber for new racks for the barrels that will be arriving soon," he said trying to think of a way to bring up the missing money.

Katie's eyes narrowed and she frowned. The memories of Eloise getting mad because he'd forgotten to ask her to go to town with him, returned. Obviously, he'd not learned his lesson. And now his current wife was going to be upset with him.

"It would have been nice to know you were going to town. There might have been some things I'm needing or I might even like to go with you," she said.

He frowned, knowing once again he'd not thought of his wife. "Would you like to go?"

She shook her head, walking towards the kitchen. "No, thank you. But I will create a list of items I need and could you please go to the post office for me. I have two letters to mail."

"Of course," he said feeling guilty. "How about if I promise the next time I'm going into town we'll make a day of it?"

She smiled. "I'd love that."

Now he was back in semi-good graces, when moments before he'd worried she had taken the money. But if she wasn't going to town with him, what would she do with the cash if she stole it? Could she be mailing it to someone in one of those letters or both?

But what if she had nothing to do with the missing money?

"Someone has been in the petty cash," he said blurting it out, hoping to see her reaction.

She turned from making her list, her brows raised to stare at him. "And you think it was me?"

"I don't know what to believe, but almost a hundred dollars is missing from the cash box," he said knowing this wasn't going well for him. Why did it seem that since their wedding night, he'd done one wrong thing after another and still she hadn't yelled at him, but quietly gotten her point across.

She shook her head. "I don't even know where you keep the cash box. Do you need money? I brought fifty dollars with me in case I needed to return to Lawrenceville. I'd be happy to give it to you."

Eloise would have screamed and yelled at him. But Katie smiled, and then shot an arrow of logic straight into his heart that made him realize he'd screwed up. The woman was kind and logical, and damn, but that hurt worse. He could tune out a raised voice, but that smile of hers twisted him in knots.

Now he really was the worst husband ever. His wife was offering to give him money when she learned someone had stolen his cash. And he knew she couldn't have much or she would never have become a mail-order bride.

"Thanks, but there are more funds in the bank. I just hadn't planned on stopping there today," he said.

"You're welcome to use my cash, if you need to," she said giving him a big smile.

"That's okay," he just wanted to get going. "I know we need to talk, but if you don't mind, I want to get on the road."

He leaned down and kissed her on the cheek. "See you tonight."

"Sure," she said. "Just don't wait too long, Daniel. Secrets should never be between a husband and wife."

~

When the back door to the kitchen opened, Katie looked up from cleaning to see a strange man enter. He removed his hat. "Mrs. O'Malley, Jack Edwards, foreman, Mrs. O'Malley. Is Mr. O'Malley around?"

A curl of uneasiness spiraled through Katie, but she drew her shoulders back and smiled at him. "I'm sorry, but he's gone into town. I'm surprised he didn't say something to you. He went for lumber for the new racks he's going to build."

"Oh, that's right. I completely forgot."

She wanted him to leave. Her husband didn't want men in the house while he was gone and she didn't need Mother O'Malley telling Daniel he'd been here. She would tell him when he came home.

"I've heard you're doing a lot to the old house. Are you certain the first Mrs. O'Malley would approve?"

Katie gazed at the man her uneasiness growing. "If you're referring to Eloise, she's dead."

"Yes, I know. But what about the older Mrs. O'Malley?"

What was the man trying to say to her? What was he doing? "As Mr. O'Malley's wife, I am in charge of the household. Is there something else you need?"

Katie wanted him out of here.

"I just wanted to check on Mr. O'Malley. Nice to meet you, ma'am."

"Yes, you too," she said and watched him go out the same door he'd come in. He didn't even knock, but rather just opened the door and came in. He was probably a perfectly nice man, but she didn't want anyone just opening the door and walking in.

An hour later the kitchen door opened again and her handsome husband walked through the doorway. He hadn't been gone as long as she'd expected.

"You're home early."

Funny normally she didn't see much of him during the day, but just knowing he wasn't out in the fields, she'd missed him more today than usual. But after her guest, she was glad to see Daniel home.

"It didn't take as long as I thought," he said kissing her on the cheek. He glanced around the room. "It looks so much better. Just cleaning it made the difference?"

"I did rearrange the cabinets a little and gave everything a good scrubbing. In the spring, I'd like to start giving the walls a fresh coat of paint," she said, pushing back a stray lock of hair that had fallen onto her face.

"How's Mother been today?"

What could she say? Your mother is a mean-spirited woman who I've tried to be nice to, but I'm reaching the end of my reserves? Or did she just nod her head?

"Good. She's been in her room most of the day, but that was because I threatened to let her help me with the cleaning."

He laughed. "You're good for her."

Katie smiled. "Feeling sorry for yourself only brings yourself and everyone around you down. I want our home to be a happy place for us and our children."

If they ever had children. She kept reminding herself that she should allow her husband his rights if she wanted babies. And yet, she wasn't quite ready. Soon.

Pulling her into his arms, he stared down at her. "I think we should get started on creating these babies."

Feeling his body against hers, felt right. Spirals of warmth were trickling through her and she laid her head on his shoulder. "In time."

She leaned back in his arms. "I better get busy or you won't have any supper." She stepped out of his arms. "I need to tell you that I had a visitor this afternoon."

"Who?"

"Your foreman, Jack Edwards, came through the back door without knocking. Does he normally do this?"

Daniel frowned. "He's never done it while I'm here."

"Maybe he got confused because he was looking for you."

"Maybe," Daniel said. "I told him I was going into town."

"I wanted to tell you since I knew how you felt about me being alone in the house with a man. He stayed about five minutes. He asked to see the changes to the house that I was making, but I told him today was not a good day."

"Thank you," he said.

"He's a strange man."

"But he knows vineyards and that's why he's here."

Maybe he was good with wine, but right now, Katie felt weird with him around.

"I better get started on supper."

"Oh," he reached back behind him and pulled some envelopes out of his back pocket. "These were at the post office for you."

Taking the envelopes from his hand, her heart started to race and she squealed. "It's letters from Genny and Julia."

Quickly she stepped away from him, sank down in a chair and ripped the first envelope open and began to read.

November 1, 1890

Dear Katie and Julia,

I hope you don't mind that I made the letter to the two of you. I also hope that this reaches you and finds you both well and happy.

My new husband, Stuart MacDonnell, is kind and very handsome. I couldn't figure out why a man like him would send for a mail-order bride. He said he needed someone quickly and didn't want to have to court someone for two years and pretend to be in love. I suppose that makes sense, but it seems to do so to him.

I don't know if I believe him or not. But he didn't waste any time marrying me. It happened in a judge's office about thirty minutes after I arrived.

Stuart told me he doesn't want any more children. Had I known before I wouldn't have come, but he does have two beautiful children that I've fallen completely in love with. Three-year old Billy is a rascal and adorable. He has blond hair like his mother and his father's gorgeous blue eyes.

Lucy is six-months old and the most wonderful baby I've ever known. She took my heart as soon as I saw her. She has brown hair that's in soft curls all over her head and again her father's blue eyes. She's so funny. Babbles all the time and laughs like she's just told you a funny story.

And that's my new family. I already adore them, including I'm afraid, their father. If he would just let me in, we'd have such a wonderful marriage and a good life. I don't know what I'm going to do if he won't let me in. I don't know if I can live in a situation without love or at least the possibility of gaining it someday.

I keep telling myself that it's all right. I don't need love. But it's a lie. I do need it to survive. I need it for my very soul to be nourished and happy.

Thank you both for letting me carry-on so, though I know you didn't have any say about it. I miss you both so much and hope you have found the loves of your life and that they love you back.

I guess that's the problem. I have found the love of my life and he doesn't love me back.

I hope to hear from you both soon.

My love to you both,
Genny
After Katie had read the first one, she sighed and ripped open the second letter, from Julia.
Dear Katie and Genny,
My dearest friends, I already miss both of you so much. I have arrived safely in Wickerton, New York. I wish I could tell you it went smoothly, but unfortunately, my intended groom took an issue with my limp.
I was mortified to have him leave me at the train station, with the poor sheriff stuck having to tell me Mr. Johnson didn't wish to marry me, after all.
Since that time I have come to be rather grateful the man didn't want to marry me. The sheriff has been kind enough to give me a job at the jailhouse until I can find other employment.
Please know that my love and thoughts are with you both.
Love,
Julia
Katie choked up as tears pricked her lids. Poor Julia had suffered so much due to an unfortunate accident that left her with a limp. She worried about the poor girl and if she could, she would immediately send for her and find some type of work for her here.

But that was impossible, given the state of her marriage to Mr. O'Malley. Hopefully it would soon improve and then she would invite her friend to come to Charlottesville. But if not, she could be joining her in the near future.

Chapter Six

Katie sat next to her husband at the dinner table that night, her mother-in-law across from her. She'd been civil all day and Katie hoped they could get through one meal without her starting something new or revealing another of Daniel's secrets.

She was tired from cleaning, though in the last two weeks she had worked until the house sparkled from top to bottom. Now she was going to start on going through the linens.

"When do you think you'll start selling the cabernet?" his mother asked.

She seemed better today. There was a calmness that had been missing before and Katie wondered about her. What had changed besides Katie talking to her?

"Anytime. I think the first batch of wine is ready. Katie and I had part of a bottle the other night."

"Who will be your customers," Katie asked.

There was so much about Daniel's business she wanted to know. She wanted to understand what her husband loved about creating his own wine. They'd been married less than a month and she was still learning about her husband, both the good and the bad.

"Restaurants, clients, and liquor stores. I'd really like to get a distribution deal that would ship our wines across the country."

"Have you named the wine?"

"O'Malley's," he said quietly. "This way I can just name the type of wine and people will know it came from our vineyard."

"Well, Mr. O'Malley, I think you have overlooked one big possible client."

"Who?"

"The Catholic church. Wine is used every Sunday at mass. You might want to see who supplies their wine. It seems to me that supporting a local vineyard would certainly be better than hauling the stuff from the liquor store."

"That's a great suggestion."

An idea begin to form in her mind and she could barely sit still from the excitement. From what she could see, Daniel had very little interaction with the people of Charlottesville and that had to change.

"I think that we need a party to debut our wine. We could not only serve it, but give everyone a small taste of what we're doing here at O'Malley's Vineyards."

His mother made a hrrmphing sound that she couldn't tell was for or against her idea.

"No one would attend and you know why," she said glancing at her son, her brows raised.

Daniel, cut his meat and placed a bite in his mouth. While he chewed, Katie could see the wheels turning in his head. "You don't know that, Mother. They may come out of curiosity."

What were they discussing? It was like they were talking a secret language only they understood. This probably had to do with Eloise.

"They may attend because they heard you have a new wife," Katie said. She knew what she was doing. She was urging her husband to come and talk to her, let her know his past. But so far that had not happened. And with each passing day, she grew more curious.

She watched her husband contemplating her idea. "The holidays will soon be here. We could make it a Christmas party. Decorate the house, food, company and introduce my beautiful wife to the community."

"And launch your new wine," she said. "We could give our guests a gift when they left, a bottle of Chardonnay."

Katie didn't know if the Chardonnay was ready, but it was a suggestion. A taste of their wine. A chance for the vineyard to finally start to be profitable in the coming year.

His mother sat back watching the two of them shaking her head. "If you'll excuse me. I'm going to bed. Just the thought of a party, tires me."

While Katie cleared the table, she thought of all the preparation and how much time she would need. For their first big social event, she wanted everything to be just right.

Her husband came into the kitchen carrying dishes. "You don't have to do that. I know you're tired."

"I know."

After he helped her clear off the table, he pulled her to the parlor and sat her down. "Are you certain you want to hold a party? I mean the house is looking better than ever, but I know it's a lot of work."

"It's all right. I can't wait to meet other people in the community. I want to be your partner and help your business. I want to be a good wife to you," she said reaching out and taking his hand. "But you have to help me. You have to be honest with me."

Maybe tonight he would finally tell her about Eloise's death. She'd given him time, she'd been patient. But her resolve not to badger him was beginning to wane. He would do well to tell her. Now. Tonight.

He pulled his hand from her, stood and walked away. "You don't understand."

"I'm trying, help me."

"Eloise's death was shocking. It's in the past. I don't want to talk about it."

Katie stood and went to her husband. She laid her palm on his arm. "I have high hopes for this marriage. When I came here I wanted to create a union with a man I didn't know. I hope to have children with you and for us to have a life filled with bad and good times. But it's all based on trust and you don't trust me. You showed me that this morning, when you thought I had stolen money."

"I'm trying to trust you. But I trusted my first wife and I shouldn't have." Daniel ran his hand through his hair. "I don't like talking about Eloise because everyone in town thinks I murdered her."

He turned and walked away, leaving Katie staring at his retreating back. She sank onto the sofa. Her stomach clenched with fear and she gazed at the man she had grown to like and even care about. Could he have killed his first wife? What made people think he was her killer?

~

At daylight, Daniel woke to find his wife's side of the bed empty. Rolling over he was shocked at how quickly their marriage had spiraled into trouble. All marriages had peaks and valleys, but they were still newlyweds and they were having issues.

When he'd seen her on that train platform, he thought she'd seemed like a ray of sunshine. For over a year he'd been needing someone or something to brighten his days. And Katie did. He couldn't wait to get home and see her smiling face.

In the time she'd been here, he'd even seen a change in his mother. If he were honest with himself, he was the one causing the problems in their marriage. The girl was smart enough to recognize he was not being honest.

If he didn't tell her the truth, someone sooner or later was going to give her their version and how could he blame her for getting upset. He had to find the time to tell her what happened between him and Eloise.

There was a rapid fire knock on his bedroom door. "Mr. O'Malley, wake up, sir."

He jumped out of bed and opened the door to see one of his workers, standing before him. "Sorry, to disturb you, sir, but there is a herd of cattle out in the vineyard. I need help rounding them up."

"Dear God," he said grabbing his pants. "Where the hell is Jack?"

"I don't know, sir," he said. "I saw them when I was walking to the shed."

He paid his foreman a decent salary to make certain the vineyard was protected, the hands did their work and the wine was produced. Sure Daniel was involved in all the day to day activities, but he had a foreman because the man was in charge of his workers.

"You go on and I'll catch up to you. Who the hell's cattle is it?"

"I don't know, sir," he said running down the stairs.

If they trampled the vines, he was ruined. Everything he'd worked so hard to achieve would be for naught.

"Do you need help?" Katie said appearing in the doorway.

"Yes, pull on a coat and boots and grab a blanket to shoo them away with," he said.

No, he didn't want his wife out in the vineyard herding cattle, but if the vines were trampled, they would have nothing. They all had to work to keep them from destroying their future crops.

Hours later when they returned to the house, Katie turned to him and sank down at the table. They had saved most of the vines, but there were some the cattle had not only trampled, it appeared they'd been running through his field. Thank goodness it was not his older grapes, but the newer ones and he thought he could save the cuttings, though he would have to do a lot of work.

Katie turned and stared at him. "Do not blame this one on me."

He laid his head back against the chair rest. "If only I could, because then I would know who had created the problem. My gut is telling me this was deliberate."

But who would be trying to destroy him?

She stared at him, her big eyes wide and bright. "But why? Who would want to ruin the vineyard? You're just starting to make money."

Shrugging his shoulder he shook his head. "I don't know."

"Is there anyone who wants you to fail?"

How could he answer that question? Everyone in town thought he'd murdered Eloise. Could this be a vigilante act? Someone thought they were getting even with him for murdering his wife and maybe even marrying again? It seemed farfetched.

"I don't think so," he said and glanced at her. "Thank you for helping me and the other workers. There would have been far more damage without you chasing the cattle. But I have to tell you, there were times you had me laughing as you shooed them away and other times I was holding my breath you wouldn't get hurt."

"That one heifer wanted to chase me," she said giggling. "I thought she was going to run me over."

He chuckled. "I looked up and all I could see was you running through the field, trying to get away, and that ole heifer not far behind you. Your green eyes were as wide as I've ever seen them, your hair flying out behind you."

His wife had been amazing. She was a partner, there at his side helping him save the grapes. And when that cow had been chasing her, for a moment fear had his heart racing and his legs moving at the thought of her being injured.

"Instead of vines being smashed, I feared it would be me," she said shaking her head. "But then you diverted her attention."

She leaned her head on his shoulder. "Thank you."

Placing his hand on her head, he squeezed her. "My pleasure."

Resting, they sat in comfortable silence as they realized how close they'd come to losing everything. Daniel still had to go back out and repair the hole in the fence they'd found. It looked like someone had cut his fence and his neighbor's cattle had been driven through. If his worker hadn't found the damage right away, it could have been disastrous.

Katie had been there the entire day, protecting the vines, shooing cattle away and even guarding the broken fence. And yet he didn't want to admit to her the way the town had treated him after Eloise died. How he'd kept the knowledge of her leaving him secret, not even telling Frank until the other day.

He'd loved Eloise. Sure they were different. She wanted a rich luxurious house and he couldn't give her what she wanted. He'd watched his wife flirt with other men, but never suspected her of having an affair.

Now every time he saw a man on his property, he wondered if he was the one who she'd fornicated with. And still he didn't talk to Katie. Just this morning he'd made the decision to discuss what happened with her, but now, now he didn't want to drag up the past and expose himself and his weakness to his new wife.

No man wanted to admit his wife had found someone else.

"In the past, I've made mistakes, Katie. I know I have. I don't want to repeat those same blunders with you, but I'm not ready to talk about Eloise and what happened. I blame myself. So please, give me a little more time. I know I'm asking a lot. I know you deserve to hear the truth from me. I'm just asking for a little more time."

The day had been rough and just thinking about telling Katie about his first wife was more tension that, at this moment, he didn't need. Yes, he was being selfish, but today was almost a complete disaster. Now was not the time for him to think rationally or answer her questions with a calm head.

"Will time solve the problem?"

"No. She's dead. Today has been an unpleasant day, and frankly, I just don't want to think about that problem right now. I guess, I need a break. I want to enjoy being with you. Sitting here, looking around at the wonderful changes you've made to the house. You've turned it into a home. And how you helped me save the vineyard I've worked so hard for. I just want to rest and enjoy being with my lovely wife."

Picking up his hand, she squeezed it hard. "And I enjoy being with you. But sooner or later you've got to tell me everything. As your wife, I'm entitled to know."

~

Two weeks later, Katie wore her best dress, a chiffon blue silk that accentuated her green eyes and dark hair. She felt like a princess wearing the gown and clung to her husband's arm as they made their way through the throng of people who had arrived to celebrate the holidays and their new wine.

Martha was in the kitchen filling the goblets and soon they would all toast to the new venture. Tonight Daniel had secured two new restaurants, a liquor store, and possibly the church. That one was still being discussed.

When people first arrived, she knew many of them had come to check out the newest Mrs. O'Malley, but she didn't let that deter her one bit. She still didn't know what had happened to Eloise, but her husband was a good man. Any doubts she'd had about him killing his first wife were gone.

She'd seen the hurt on his face when he mentioned her name and couldn't believe a killer would feel that emotion.

"I'm going to make certain everything is ready," she said slipping her arm from Daniel's. She walked toward the kitchen, passing Frank on her way.

Even Mother O'Malley was decked out sitting in her wheelchair, talking to people. She caught her eye when she passed and the older woman seemed happy. She even smiled at Katie as she passed.

Katie hurried into the kitchen and when she rounded the corner, she gasped at the sight. Five bottles lay broken, the wine puddling on the floor. Martha was staring at the scattered glass in horror.

"What happened?" Katie asked rushing into the room and closing the door behind her.

"I went downstairs to get another bottle and when I returned I found this glass shattered," she said almost in tears. "I don't know what happened. Who would do this?"

Uneasiness settled over Katie. No one could know about the wine being destroyed, but there was no doubt someone was deliberately trying to harm the vineyard. Whoever it was, they wanted to cast a pallor over tonight and she would not let that happen.

"The guests are waiting. I'll run down to the cellar and get more. You start opening and pouring the wine. After we serve, I'll come back and help you clean up."

"No, ma'am. You'll get your dress dirty. I can handle the cleanup I just didn't want you to think I'd done this."

The thought had crossed Katie's mind, but she'd quickly pushed it aside. Martha was too stunned to have done something like this and she would be the person cleaning it up. It didn't make sense.

She hugged the woman to her. "No, I don't think you did this, but was there anyone in the kitchen before you went downstairs?"

"No one. Whoever did this had to be quick."

"As I serve the wine, I'm going to see if anyone has wine on their clothing. I don't know how they could keep from being splattered."

Katie hurried down the wine cellar and quickly chose two more bottles. Glancing around she made sure everything downstairs was secure. Then she all but ran upstairs. When she reached the kitchen, Martha had found one bottle that they hadn't destroyed. She had one tray of glasses poured.

"I'll take this to our guests while you pour the rest."

Entering the main area of the house, she quickly passed around glasses.

"Do you need help?" Daniel asked.

"Oh no, I can handle it," she said, not wanting to ruin the party for her husband. Once he learned that someone had broken some of his best Chardonnay, she knew he would be upset. Why spoil the event he'd been looking forward to.

As she handed out the glasses, she tried her best to check everyone's clothing.

Going back into the kitchen, she took the last tray of glasses.

"Don't leave the kitchen," she warned. "If they destroy the wine in the cellar, we will be out of business."

"I'll stay right here."

Passing out the last of the wine glasses, she was no closer to knowing who had caused so much destruction than she was before. No one had wine or red stains on their clothing and everyone seemed to be in the best of spirits.

Daniel took a letter opener and clinked against the side of his goblet. "Can I have everyone's attention. I'd like to make a toast tonight to the two best things in my life. First my lovely new wife, Katie, my own ray of sunshine. She's brought new light and life into his old house and turned it into a home. And then to the O'Malley vineyard and the first Chardonnay we've produced. Thank you for being here tonight. Cheers."

Katie followed along with everyone and lifted her glass, "Cheers."

Her husband's toast was nice, but part of her wished he'd made some kind of declaration of love. But she was quickly learning that Daniel O'Malley was a kind, gentle man who didn't like showing his emotions or talking about them. She was certain that was the reason she'd yet to learn the story of Eloise's passing.

She took a sip of the wine and for the first time, she savored the different flavors and even enjoyed the tangy taste of the liquid on her tongue.

A woman adorned with jewels and a gorgeous dress, walked up to her. "Dear, I have to tell you that you have made such a difference in this house. Betty looks better, the house is beautiful and even Daniel seems happy. I'm glad he married you. He'd become such a hermit after Eloise died so tragically."

The woman was nice, but Katie didn't want to talk about Eloise. She wanted to hear from her husband what had happened. She glanced at Daniel standing in a group of men, talking.

"Why, thank you. He's made me very happy," Katie replied. Maybe she could slip away from her now.

The woman leaned in close to her. "Did you live around these parts?"

"Oh no, I'm originally from Lawrenceville, Massachusetts."

The woman drew back. "How in the world did you two meet?"

Katie glanced at her husband again. They had agreed that telling everyone she was a mail-order bride would

 Sylvia McDaniel

seem scandalous, so they'd come up with a plan that was a slight version of the truth.

"We met through mutual friends. We corresponded back and forth and finally decided to marry."

"Oh my," the woman said. "And you came to Virginia without meeting him in person? Did you know what happened to Eloise before you met him?"

Katie wanted to scream. And now she had to answer this woman's question, while wanting to get to the kitchen and check on Martha.

"Daniel explained her death and I believe him," she said. "Excuse me, I must check on the kitchen."

Hurrying away, she wished her husband would tell her his version of what had happened to Eloise, so she could answer these confusing questions. Oh, who was she kidding. She just wanted to hear the truth from his lips.

Chapter Seven

Daniel was shocked at how many people had shown up for the party. Katie's idea of blending the holidays, the debut of their Chardonnay and their wedding into one big event was a huge success. He'd feared no one would come and yet the house was full of laughter, people drinking wine, and celebrating their happiness.

All because of Katie. He watched his wife flitting from group to group, and he couldn't help but feel blessed. She'd come to Virginia, knowing nothing about him and chosen to spend the rest of her life with him.

If he could believe what people were saying, the wine was a huge success and now he just needed to push the product to more restaurants, liquor stores, and maybe enter a few competitions to see if it was as good as people were telling him.

The town banker, Joseph Bruhn walked up to him. "Excellent Chardonnay. I would like for you to send me a case, just let me know the cost. Want to get it before it's gone."

Daniel smiled. "Of course, Joseph. I'll get that delivered to your place tomorrow."

What did the man mean before it's gone? Was there a possibility of them selling out right away? Is that what people were saying. A thrill of excitement and success rushed through him.

He'd known for years he wanted to do something with his hands. Some type of farming or agricultural and when he'd read about Thomas Jefferson's vineyard in college, he knew he'd found his calling.

"All the talk I'd heard in town said you were going to be successful. That you were doing all the right things to make a good vineyard. I thought maybe you would be the one to break the curse of Thomas Jefferson."

Shocked, he stared at the banker. "I am. I hope to have the first successful winery in the state of Virginia."

"Then why are you selling?"

Stunned, Daniel stared at the banker, his heart leaping into his throat as his stomach clenched. "I'm not selling. Who told you that?"

The banker looked surprised. "Someone is double crossing someone. I have buyers coming to look over your property and see about a loan. They think the place is up for sale."

"What?"

Fear trickled up his spine and he thought about his conversation with Frank. Was he trying to sell the vineyard?

"Who told you I wanted to sell?"

"Why, Frank, of course."

Daniel clenched his fist to control the anger roaring through him.

"There's a tobacco company buying up land all over Virginia. They're coming to look at your property," the banker said, an uneasy expression on his face. "I'm sorry, Daniel. I thought you were looking for a buyer."

"I'll make you a promise. I'll contact you before I let anyone else know when I'm ready to trade. But let's just say you'll probably be making that transaction from heaven or hell, depending on where you plan on spending eternity."

Knowing it wasn't the bankers fault didn't make his anger any less, when he thought of how Frank had people coming to look at the land after he'd told him no. Daniel wasn't selling. Or at least it appeared Frank was trying to negotiate a deal on the land. If he hadn't mentioned it at dinner the other night, he might have gotten away with everything. And then what would Daniel have done?

"Again, I apologize."

"No apology necessary. But O'Malley Vineyards is not on the market. We're doing well and soon we're going to be doing great."

Anger spiraled through Daniel like a forest fire out of control. Was Frank double crossing him? Could his best friend be trying to work a deal behind his back. They'd been friends a long time. Daniel trusted him and he'd been beside him during his darkest days.

Why would he try to sell the land without Daniel's knowledge?

~

Most of the guests had left, and Daniel was saying goodbye to the last of them now. Katie carried a tray of empty wine glasses into the kitchen, pleased the party had gone so well. And that her husband had been so outgoing, friendly, and by her side most of the night, touching her in the slightest way.

The lingering feel of his hands announcing to his friends, we're together, we're happy, and I'm thrilled to be married to her. His toast had been heart warming and she'd felt cherished.

One thing about her husband, while there was a cloud of shadow and suspicion hanging over him, he was kind to her. Though adjusting to marriage had been hard for both of them.

But what happened to his first wife and why didn't he want to talk about it? Entering the hallway that led to the kitchen, she bumped into Frank. "Sorry, I was deep in thought and didn't see you there in the shadows."

"Great party," he said to her. "Everything went really well and the turnout was much better than I expected. What with the scandal, I didn't think anyone would come."

Licking her dry lips, she gazed at him, knowing he knew about the incident with Daniel's first wife. While she knew she should wait for her husband, she'd given him ample time and he'd yet to tell her about Eloise. "Tell me about the scandal. What happened."

The man was her husband's best friend, so surely he knew the story of what happened to her husband's first wife.

He stared in shock at her. "Daniel hasn't told you?"

"Daniel doesn't want to talk about it. He said some day he'd tell me, but I had several comments said tonight that concerned me. I need to know what happened."

Taking the tray from her hand, he led her into the empty kitchen. For a moment she wondered where Martha had gone. The room was empty and after the broken wine bottles she'd found earlier tonight, she feared someone breaking into the cellar and finishing the destruction of the winery. The woman was supposed to stay in the kitchen.

"The scandal concerns what happened to Eloise. Many people believe that Daniel killed her."

That much Katie knew, but she wanted to understand why people believed her husband would kill his wife and how Eloise had died.

"How?" Katie asked. "I found her death certificate and it said exposure."

"Yes," he replied setting down the tray of dirty wine goblets. "Eloise left during the night. The next morning her body was found. She was in her nightgown, barefooted without a coat. It appeared she'd left the house in a hurry. The sheriff thought maybe she was running and hit her head on a rock. There was a gash in her head and blood. Many people believed she must have been running from Daniel when she fell."

Katie felt concern and shock ripple through her as she thought of her husband sending his wife out into the cold. The man she knew would never do something so evil. "But why? He loved her, he told me so."

Shrugging, Frank faced her. "I recently learned she was expecting and he knew the baby wasn't his. So maybe there was a reason she was running."

Eloise had been pregnant? With another man's child? That must have hurt Daniel so much. The thought of the woman he loved expecting another man's child, would have devastated him.

"Maybe she left to go to her lover."

"Without her coat and shoes in the dead of winter?"

Katie glanced around at the kitchen she'd worked so hard to clean. The home she'd created here, and yet, there was this cloud of darkness she hadn't been able to dispense and now she knew the reason why. The death of Eloise hung like a ghost over the house and until Katie could somehow learn the truth, her husband would never be free of the shadows.

"Did anyone look for her coat and shoes here in the house? Maybe she was wearing them when she left and her killer – lover hid them to make it appear that Daniel was behind her death."

Frank frowned. "I'm sure the sheriff would have checked that out."

"Daniel, did not kill Eloise or send her out into the cold. Something happened that night no one is talking about and I'm going to find out and clear my husband's name."

There had to be more because she refused to believe Daniel had killed Eloise. They were missing something that would lead them to the real killer.

The door opened and Daniel walked in.

"What the hell is going on Frank? First you tell the banker I'm selling the property and now I catch you talking to my wife about Eloise? What are you doing?"

Katie jerked her head from her husband to Frank, her heart pounding in her chest.

~

Daniel had heard enough to know that Katie was defending him, telling Frank she didn't believe he had killed Eloise. He hadn't told her about the suspicions the town had, but it sounded like Frank had told his wife everything. Of his pain and humiliation at the knowledge his wife was leaving him for another man.

"We're business partners, but that doesn't give you the right to interfere in my personal life. We're friends, but that doesn't give you the right to do what you've done."

He felt betrayed that Frank would have found someone to buy the land and hadn't told him. Daniel had no intention of selling. Not when the vineyard was finally starting to see success. This had taken years and he thought his friend would help him be successful, not try to undermine his operations.

"All I've done is try to help you. I stood by you when everyone in town believed you killed Eloise. I ordered you a mail-order bride, when I thought you needed companionship and it would help your position in town. I lent you money when your damn vineyard drained you and became your partner."

Daniel knew what he said was true. Frank had been there during those terrible days right after Eloise's death. He refused to call it a murder, because he hadn't kill her. He'd loved her even though she'd been difficult. Glancing at Katie, he realized how she'd done more in the short time she was here, than Eloise had ever accomplished. She was a helpmate, a joy and his life was better with her by his side.

"You're right. You have been my friend, but why did the banker ask why I'm going to sell the property when the wine is delicious and should do very well? Why, Frank? He told me you were the one who found the buyer."

"And I told you about the buyers. I presented the opportunity to you and you declined. I forgot to tell the banker. I've already told the buyer the deal is dead."

Daniel stopped for a moment. Was this all just a big misunderstanding? Was he wrong to question what Frank was doing. He sighed and sank down into a chair. Had the attacks on the vineyard made him afraid that someone was betraying him?

Frank had always been his good friend and now he was suspicious of the man, when it wasn't his fault that someone was deliberately sabotaging the wine. "There for a moment I thought you were double crossing me. "

"Have I ever double crossed you? We've been friends a long time, you're more a brother than a friend. I would never do anything that could hurt you or Katie. You're my family. Even your old crotchety mother I care about," Frank said his eyes flashing with rage at Daniel.

"Well, this has certainly been a very revealing night," Katie replied, placing her hands on her hips. "On the night of our very first successful party, Frank, not you, my darling husband, tells me about the death of your first wife."

A ripple of *oh crap, I'm in so much trouble* had Daniel's stomach clenching, his breath swooshing from his chest. From the tone of her voice, his lovely wife was furious. He'd never seen her so angry before and then he realized with startling clarity she just learned the truth regarding Frank ordering him a mail-order bride.

"You, Daniel O'Malley, didn't order a mail-order bride, Frank did. Now it's all starting to come together. But why did you marry me?"

"Katie, let me explain."

She walked out of the room, leaving him staring at the door.

"I think I will leave you two to sort this out. There has been enough discord between us tonight. I'd like to remain friends and partners without remembering this night as the time I ended your marriage. I'll show myself out the door."

Frank left the kitchen, his boots echoing on the wooden floor. In the silence that followed, Daniel heard the front door of the house open and close. He hurried out of the room to find his wife. He had to right this wrong now.

He found her in the parlor sitting on the sofa, crying. His chest ached with the pain he'd caused this lovely young woman. She deserved a much better husband than him. She deserved to be happy and when he married her, he'd only thought of himself. Yet he didn't want to let her go. He desperately wanted to make this marriage work.

Sitting, he pulled her reluctant stiff body into his arms. He wanted to hold her, soothe her and let her know she'd been the best thing that had ever happened to him.

"After Eloise's death, I had no intentions of ever marrying again. When I went to Frank's office, I told him I would not marry you and planned on sending you back on the next train to Lawrenceville.

"But then I saw you and you were a ray of sunshine I couldn't turn away. I didn't even consider not marrying you. I took you to the county courthouse and made you my wife.

"Don't be angry with me for not being the one who wrote to you. I wanted you from the moment I saw you. Frank may have brought us together, but I chose to make you my wife."

Standing, Katie walked away, her shoulders were heaving and he knew she was crying. Rising from the sofa, he walked up behind her, he turned her in his arms and saw the tears flowing down her cheeks. The sight filled his chest with a pain he'd never felt. He didn't want to make her cry.

Pulling her in his arms, he whispered against her head, "I know I'm not an easy man to live with and I've made mistakes, but don't give up on me. No, I didn't intend to marry you that day, but I'm so glad I did."

How could he convince her his life was so enriched because she was here. And now he couldn't imagine his living without her.

"I want to believe you. I really do, but it's hard with all of the allegations I keep hearing."

"Believe that these last few weeks with you have made me happier than I can remember. Believe that I want us to have children and grow old together. I want you working beside me in our vineyard, making our family business a success. I want you to be my partner for life. "

When the words came out of his mouth he was shocked and yet they were true. Besides the party, which had been her idea, he'd not included her in the decisions and the running of the vineyard. Maybe it was time to show her how important she was to him. Maybe it was time to court his lovely wife and make her feel a part of the operation. Maybe it was time to treat her with the respect his wife was due.

"Come to bed, Katie. Whether or not you sleep with me doesn't matter. I'd just like to hold and comfort you and show you how much I care about you."

Tugging on her hand he led her from the kitchen and into the hall towards the stairs and their bedroom.

Chapter Eight

Katie awoke the next morning feeling more confused than ever. The Christmas party had been a huge success and the debut of the wine had them giddy over its success. Now if only the orders would come pouring in.

Last night had been illuminating in so many ways with Katie learning about Eloise's death and the banker telling Daniel about the buyer for the vineyard. So much had happened, but the most confusing of all had been her husband.

For a man people believed had killed his first wife, he'd been kind and caring last night when she'd learned he had not been the one behind the ad in the Grooms' Gazette, but Frank.

And yet when they'd gone to bed, he'd simply held her until she fell asleep. She'd been so exhausted, once her head hit the pillow, she quickly slipped off into dreamland where none of the pressing problems of the day were present.

Somehow she wanted to find out who had really killed Eloise. Sure, her husband must have been in pain at the idea of his wife, pregnant with another man's child, leaving him. But he didn't seem capable of hurting someone he loved. He'd taken care of his cranky mother for the last five years and Katie couldn't help but think anyone who would do that woman, deserved a box of gold nuggets.

Katie climbed out of bed and stretched. Hurriedly she dressed. The cock had crowed, the sun was up and she was late getting downstairs. The smell of bacon hit her nose as she reached the kitchen. Opening the door, she saw her mother-in-law sitting at the table drinking tea and her husband cooking eggs.

"Good morning," he said. "I hope you rested well."

"Sorry, I'm late. I slept so hard last night that I overslept this morning."

He came around the kitchen table and kissed her softly on the mouth. "You worked so hard on that party, I'm sure you were exhausted."

His mother smiled. "It was a good party. I enjoyed it."

Praise from his mother? Had the sun risen in the west or had Katie just not totally awakened yet? Was she dreaming. "I'm glad you had a good time, Mother O'Malley."

"Well, don't let it go to your head. People still don't like my son."

All the revelations from last night suddenly weighed heavy on Katie's heart and she couldn't help but wonder why so many people had attended their event. Was it curiosity or something else? And who had destroyed all the wine bottles last night? It had to be someone at the party. Or could it have been Martha? The woman had disappeared when she'd asked her to stay.

"Mother," Daniel warned. "Katie is not responsible for how people perceive me. It was her idea for the party and we have reason to celebrate this morning."

Warmth rushed through her clear down to her center. Last night her husband had held her gently in his arms and this morning he was defending her to his mother.

Were his words last night true? She hoped so, because she could still see so much potential here and she felt so much hope that maybe they were finally coming together as a couple. Maybe they could put the past behind them.

"I'll finish breakfast," she said moving towards the stove. "No, I'm cooking this morning and then I'd like to take you for a buggy ride around the property. I want to show you what you're a part of," he said gazing at her, his blue eyes sparkling with warmth.

"Yes," she said breathlessly. "I'd love to spend some time seeing the vineyard and be with you."

"But I wanted you to read to me this afternoon. We haven't finished Tom Sawyer. I have to know if they found him."

Daniel raised his brows and gave his mother a hard look. "Mother."

Katie smiled at her husband, her heart in her throat. While she didn't want the two of them fighting over her, it felt good when her husband put his mother in her place.

"Fine, but I get her later. She's going to read to me."

Katie smiled. Suddenly she felt like things were different between all of them. Even his mother seemed to have accepted Katie into their family. "We'll read later this afternoon."

His mother sighed, but when Daniel turned his back, she frowned at Katie. Well, maybe things weren't perfect, but at least they'd made progress and now if only she could help her husband be accepted by the community.

Later that morning as Daniel tucked a blanket around her legs to keep her warm, she gazed at her husband and smiled. "What a wonderful day to get out of the house for a while. I feel like I've been inside for weeks."

And she had. She'd spent the days since she'd arrived, cleaning the house, organizing the rooms, and becoming the lady of the house. Even when some people didn't want her to take on that role. Daniel frowned. "You know you can take the buggy into town any time you want to go."

"No, I didn't know. I would like to get involved with the women from church. I think I'll host a tea for them before the holidays. A sort of come out and get to know me, event," she said gazing at her husband.

"We just had the Christmas party? Are you sure you want to do this so soon?"

She smiled and patted him on the arm. "This would just be for the ladies of the church. No one else."

He clicked to the horses and the buggy lurched forward. "All right. I guess I can see how women would enjoy that."

Katie wanted to belong to the community. Daniel needed her help once again be a part of the society of Charlottesville.

"I also think it would be good for you mother. I think one of the reasons she can be trying is that she's bored. What does she do all day but think about her troubles. We need to give her things to do. Even if it's just small things. What if you asked her to embroider you some handkerchiefs or dishtowels."

Daniel started laughing. "You want her to yell at me?"

"No, I just thought if you asked her, she would feel needed. You're her son. You no longer require her help, but she loves you and wants to be a part of your life," Katie said softly. "Think of how you'll feel when our children are grown and leave us."

She could see the years rolling by and she wanted to make certain she was here for it all. Unlike the way hers had been cut short with her family.

Glancing at her, he smiled. "I can't wait to have children with you."

Katie grinned. "Me, too."

Urging the horses forward, he said, "Let me show you the vineyard you're a partner in, Mrs. O'Malley."

The feel of his hand laying on her thigh and the words warmed her enough the blanket covering her legs felt hot, but she didn't remove it for fear the wind would chill her. How could they have children if she never laid with her husband? And why did she suddenly feel the urge to try again with him. Would it be better this time?

∼

After touring the vineyard, Katie was ready to come in out of the blustery cold wind and spend the afternoon with Mother O'Malley. Her husband had things he needed to handle and yet before they parted, he kissed her soundly.

It was the kind of kiss a girl dreamed of and a woman relished. It was the kind of kiss that had her longing for the evening when she would spend time alone with her husband. Both of them wanted the same things, a family and a way to support the brood of children they longed for. The business was growing and expanding and now they were working towards the children.

Christmas was only three weeks away and she couldn't help but think how wonderful it would be if she conceived during the holidays. Time would tell.

Pulling off her coat and scarf, she hung them up in the closet and pulled on her apron as she walked into the parlor.

The thump thump thump of the wheelchair let her know her mother-in-law was headed in her direction. Katie sank on the sofa to await her. She picked up a stack of Daniel's shirts she wanted to repair before he came home tonight.

"You're back," she said rolling into the room a disgruntled expression on her face.

With trepidation Katie realized, the woman was not in the best of spirits.

"Yes, I just came in a few minutes ago. Would you like some hot tea?"

"No, I'm fine. I thought maybe you could read to me this afternoon."

Certainly. Let me finish this piece of mending," she said.

The woman became exasperated and yelled. "Hurry up, girl. I've been waiting all day for you."

Everything centered around this woman and Katie wondered if it had been this way all her life or only since the accident. If she had ever acted this way with the nuns, they would have taken the rod to her and made her go to confession. She knew her mother-in-law was lonely, but still there was no point in acting so selfish.

Katie smiled and continued to work on sewing the rip in a shirt. "I realize you have nothing to keep you occupied. I was thinking maybe you could help me with the mending. Two hands make the job go by faster."

"I hate sewing."

That was obvious. It was the one household duty her mother-in-law could have easily done and yet she refused to even consider helping. Instead she preferred other people to take care of her.

"I enjoy taking a piece of material and creating something new and exciting from the cotton. When you finish it gives you such a feeling of accomplishment," Katie responded trying to remain positive and not let her destroy the warm feelings from the morning.

How wretched to spend the last years of her life unhappy and doing everything she could to make everyone around her miserable.

"Hrumph. I don't need a feeling of accomplishment. I'm an old woman, just waiting to die."

Setting her sewing down, Katie looked at her mother-in-law. "How can you say that. That's so wrong."

"But it's true."

Misery loves company and somehow Katie felt like her mother-in-law wanted everyone around her to be unhappy.

"Only because you make yourself be this mean, nasty woman people don't like. Since the day I walked into this house, you have been disrespectful and hateful to me. I've put up with your disposition thinking it would eventually change, but it hasn't.

"I thought maybe it was because you didn't like to share Daniel, but I don't believe that anymore. I think you like being considered a snide, mean old woman, it keeps people away. They don't have to see the hurt and the pain inside you, just waiting to die."

Daniel's mother stared at her in shock, her mouth wide open.

Katie rose from the sofa. She'd gone too far. She shouldn't have been so truthful with her mother-in-law and somehow kept her mouth shut. But she'd had enough.

What started out as a great morning, celebrating their party and seeing the vineyard had quickly become frustrating. "Excuse me, but I think there are more pressing matters for me to do this afternoon. I don't feel like being yelled at any more."

Walking out of the room, wanting only to escape and prepare herself for her evening with Daniel, she heard her mother-in-law crying.

Whirling around, she stared in disbelief as the old woman bent her head and sobbed.

"Oh my God," Katie realized she'd lost her smile. She let the woman's meanness get to her instead of smiling. She ran to her chair. "I'm so sorry. I was wrong to say that to you."

The old woman sniffed. "No, you were right. I know I'm mean and nasty, but...it's not the physical pain that troubles me. I've learned to live with that. It's the fact that I lived in that horrible buggy accident and my dear, sweet husband, Bartholomew didn't."

She started crying again, big heaving sobs that tore at Katie's heart. "Would he want to see you suffering like this? Would he want to hear you being so crass with everyone? Daniel misses his sweet mother. He's told me so."

"I know, but why didn't I die with Bart or why isn't he here sitting in this chair?"

"I understand why you wanted to die with Bart, but would you want him to suffer like you?"

Katie could see the pain on the woman's face. She could see the guilt of living while her husband had died. Her chest ached with the knowledge of how that must pain the woman.

"Of course not," she said with a sniffle.

"Do you think he would want you to live your life this way?"

"That's too easy," she said with a laugh. "I know he wouldn't because he always took me aside, when he thought I was being too critical."

Katie smiled. "It can't be easy losing your husband in an accident. I can't begin to imagine the pain. I lost my entire family in the yellow fever epidemic of 1880."

Betty reached out and grasped her hand. "I didn't know."

"After they died, I was sent to an orphanage where the sisters told me I should feel blessed to be alive. I had lived because God had a purpose for my life.

"Every time I cried to feel pity for myself or them, Sister Katherine would make me work. Not to forget my loved ones, but to keep me busy. The sisters taught me to work through my grief. You, dear Mother, have no work. We need to get your hands and your mind working."

Looking back, Katie knew she would have died if she hadn't been sent to the orphanage. Not because she was a child, but because she grieved her family so much, she would have been consumed by the sorrow.

"That's a touching story, but Bartholomew was the better person. I should have died and he should have lived."

"Who are you to doubt why the good Lord took him away? Or maybe you're being given a second chance to be the kind of person Bartholomew was?"

The question of why her brother and little sister died had troubled Katie for years, they were younger, they were so sweet and yet they were in heaven and she was here on earth. But she believed their presence lived on through her. "Christmas is coming. What if we make cookies and mail them to the orphanage, where I grew up. The kids love baked goods and seldom get them. You need to focus on helping other people. You lived for a reason."

Silence filled the parlor and Katie feared she'd said too much. Her mother-in-law wiped the tears from her face and then gazed at Katie, but she couldn't tell what the woman was thinking.

"Katie O'Malley, I've done everything I could to run you off and you refuse to go. Instead, you've made my son a fine wife and now you're helping me. I'm glad you're my daughter-in-law."

Relief filled Katie. She knew there would still be times they disagreed, but maybe, just maybe, they would now get along and have peace.

"Thank you. Now, would you like to have me finish Tom Sawyer?"

She dabbed her eyes and smiled. "Yes, and hand me some of that mending. I could sew while you read."

Katie felt warmth rush into her chest. It had taken longer than she'd expected, but she thought her mother-in-law had finally accepted her. She smiled and picked up the book.

~

After dinner, Mother O'Malley retired to bed, pleading she was tired, leaving Daniel alone with Katie. At the table, his mother had been friendly, even cordial, and he'd wondered what had transpired during the day to make his mother be nice for a change.

His wife glanced out the window and then turned to him, her green eyes wide with excitement. "It's snowing."

Laughing, he stoked the fire in the fireplace, throwing another log onto the blaze. Katie oozed happiness and giddiness at the same time. She was a breath of fresh air in a stale room. "It's December. It usually snows."

"We're going to have a white Christmas," she said excited, a smile on her face, dancing around like a child.

He had to go into town and pick her up something special for Christmas. He didn't know what, but it would be their first holiday together and he wanted her to remember it fondly. He'd never gotten around to giving her a wedding ring, so he'd look to see if there was one he could afford.

Rising from the fireplace, he took her by the hand drew her to the sofa. Sinking down, her skirts billowed around them. "What did you do to my mother today? She's different."

"What do you mean?" Katie said with that impish grin that drew him to her. He wanted to kiss her dimples, her lips, her eyes. He wanted to carry her up to bed, but he was going to do things the right way this time. Slow and steady with her right beside him every step of the way until they both received satisfaction.

"She smiled during dinner. She talked."

Katie took his hand and brought it to her lips. "It was amazing. When I came back from being with you, she was her usual mean self and I stood up to her. I had planned on reading to her this afternoon and when she was ugly, I told her I'd had enough of her being nasty to me." Katie sighed. "Did you realize your mother feels guilty for living while your father died in the accident? Did you know she was just waiting to die?"

Daniel stared at his wife, his chest tightening with gratitude. "I had no idea. But it wasn't her fault. And it's been years ago."

Thinking back he always believed she'd turned ugly because she was in pain and suffering because of the injuries she sustained when the buggy flipped. He'd thought her pain was physical, not mental. And he knew there was no way to cure the mental anguish except with time and love.

"She's felt remorseful all this time for living, while your father died. She pushes people away so they won't get close to her. I told her about my parents dying and how the nuns made me believe I had been blessed to live through the epidemic that took my family.

"They told me I was to do good. And I recommended she get busy helping others. After the tea with the ladies from church, we're going to send cookies to the orphanage. I want your mother to realize how blessed she is to still be living and that your father lives on through her."

Daniel swallowed, overcome that this little sprite of a woman had helped his mother. He felt like kicking himself because he'd never thought of her feeling guilty for the death of his father. The accident had been while he was away at college.

His father's death had devastated him and his mother, but he'd never realized she hadn't gotten over the tragedy of that terrible day.

He reached down and covered her mouth with his, kissing her with all the pent up passion that had built the last few weeks for this woman. Watching her standing on that platform he'd made the decision to marry her and it'd been the best decision he'd ever made.

She broke away from his kiss and smiled at him that sly grin that he adored.

"Thank you, Katie," he said.

"For what?"

"For coming into our family. For marrying me," he said, feeling his chest tighten with an emotion he'd only felt once before. The urge to carry her up the stairs and into their bedroom overwhelmed him, but he had to take his time.

Standing she held out her hand. "We should go to bed," she whispered. "I'm cold and want my husband to warm me like only he can."

Warmth spread through Daniel like a raging fire.

Daniel knew he was being given a second chance and he intended to use this opportunity to make his wife realize just how much he craved her touch. If she wasn't smiling in the morning, then he needed to give up. But he had no doubts that tonight, he would make certain she experienced pleasure.

Chapter Nine

At breakfast, the next morning, Katie smiled at her husband, who sat at the head of the table. Last night had been absolutely incredible. For the first time in her life, she felt like a desirable woman all because her husband had showed her how good it could be between the two of them.

Gazing at him this morning, her heart swelled with an emotion that could only be love. She loved this man who had been so eager that first night that he'd forgotten to take his time.

After they'd made love the first time last night, they'd cuddled and laughed about how uncomfortable that first night had been. They hadn't known each other and the experience had been clumsy and awkward.

But now, now she could hardly sit beside her man without wanting him to touch her in some small way. And she couldn't wait for tonight when they'd be alone and once again she'd find herself wrapped in his embrace.

Daniel said very little this morning, but he kept staring at her, a big smile across his handsome face. One that she wanted to trace with her fingertip.

His mother gazed at her and then at him. "You guys rest well last night?"

"Great," Daniel said gazing at Katie.

If the man didn't stop looking at her like that, his mother was going to know what they were thinking. A blush rose in her cheeks and she quickly looked away, but she couldn't stop gazing at her man.

"Wonderful," Katie said smiling at her husband. "What do you have planned for today in the vineyard?"

"I'm going to repair more of the damage to the vines from the cattle and then we're going to build racks for the new barrels I'm expecting. What about you?"

"I was going to have your mother help me. I thought we could bake some cookies. Later we might put them in tins and take them to town and give them to shut-ins. Plus the ladies from church are coming for tea tomorrow, so it will be good to have fresh cookies for them."

It would be hard to work today without dreaming of being with Daniel again. She wanted to spend time with her husband, her lover and no one else.

His mother looked at Daniel a questioning look in her eyes. "You seem happy, son."

Katie almost giggled out loud and Daniel shot her a laughing glance.

"I am. Why wouldn't I be, Mother. I have a beautiful wife who pleases me very much, the vineyard is doing well, and things seem to finally be going my way."

She nodded. "It seems that way, son."

Katie stared across the table at her husband and knew in that moment, she'd fallen in love with this handsome man. Tears pricked her eyelids and she quickly swallowed trying to hold back the flood of emotion.

Coming to Charlottesville, she'd been afraid, but at this moment, even with the question of doubt hanging over Daniel's head, she knew she loved Daniel O'Malley. Sometime during the last six weeks she'd fallen in love with this man.

Early on they'd both made mistakes in the relationship but still his words filled her with warmth and made her realize, he was a good man and she loved him. For Christmas, she wished she could clear his name somehow, but if that wasn't possible, she would do everything she could to help him with the vineyard.

She'd lost her family at such a young age, and now, she had a husband and a mother once again. The season would be perfect if they were to learn they were going to have a child.

Tonight she'd tell him she loved him.

~

After Daniel left for the vineyard, her mother-in-law and she started on the cookies. Katie mixed the dough and Betty rolled her chair to the table and cut the flattened dough using the cookie cutters Katie had found in the kitchen.

"My son seems very happy with you," she said, not looking up at Katie.

"Good, he makes me happy," Katie said, her thoughts drifting to last night. Her husband had more than made up for her disappointing wedding night. "I wonder about him and Eloise. Why wasn't she happy here?"

"She wanted Daniel to sell the vineyard and go to work for her father. Her daddy was wealthy and she expected Daniel to give her a big fancy house with servants. She didn't help my son. Not like you."

"Did they fight?"

"She liked to scream at Daniel, but he would go outside until she was ready to talk." Betty leaned back in her wheelchair and gazed at the cookie cutouts. "I haven't done this since Daniel was a little boy. It's kind of fun, but tiring."

"Did the law think Daniel killed Eloise?" Katie asked.

His mother stiffened. "Yes, but they couldn't prove it. There was not enough evidence to convict him. Don't ever believe it if someone tells you Daniel killed her. I don't know what happened to Eloise that night, but she was cheating on my son. I saw her."

How hard for her prideful man to learn from his mother that his wife had a lover. And she was dead.

Katie sighed and continued to roll out the dough. "Who was she cheating with? It would seem that would be who the sheriff should have gone after, not Daniel."

"The sheriff thought I was protecting my son." The older woman shook her head. "I don't know who she was with that night, but I've always suspected our foreman."

"Jack? No," Katie said. "He's married."

A shiver passed through her. Maybe the foreman was a really nice guy, but something about him scared her.

"Doesn't matter to some men," Betty said, shaking her head. "I've never liked that man since that day."

"Well, I can't say I've been impressed with him. First the way he came into the house when Daniel was gone. The way he wasn't here when the cattle came through the fence into the vineyard. Daniel says he knows wine, but he doesn't know how to run a vineyard."

Betty laughed and Katie turned toward her. "What's so funny?"

"You, my dear. You're very protective of my son. It's one of the things I like about you," she said.

"Well, of course, I am, he's my husband," Katie said. "There's something you said to me, when I first arrived that disturbed me."

"I've said a lot of bad things since you arrived."

"Yes, but this one was about cheating. You said I would cheat on Daniel. I want you to understand, I will *never* do that to my husband."

Betty reached out and grabbed her hand. "I know, dear. I believe you."

Katie squeezed her hand back. "Good. Daniel doesn't deserve to be treated that way."

"Thank you. No, he doesn't." The older woman sighed. "I will rest while you bake the cookies and then I'll help you decorate them."

"Good idea. I'll put the next batch in the oven. You go."

The thump, thump, thump of her wheels rolling down the hall left Katie alone in the kitchen. Hurriedly, she washed the dishes, hoping to finish before the first tray of cookies came out of the oven.

A loud knock on the door drew her attention. When she reached the door, she glanced out the window and saw Frank's carriage sitting outside. She opened the door. "Good morning, Frank. Is Daniel expecting you?"

"Katie, can I come in. I need to speak with you."

"Of course," she said, opening the door. "I'll send for Daniel."

He halted her arm. "No, don't."

"I only want to speak with you."

A trickle of alarm spiraled down her spine. Daniel had asked her not to let any men come into the house and to always let him know, but this was his friend. There was an urgency in his voice that she responded to.

"Of course, please have a seat," she said, sinking in the chair opposite Frank.

"I know you think it's probably strange that I drove out here to talk to you, but I learned some new information late yesterday and it kept me awake all night. Finally, I decided I had to come warn you."

Katie stared at her husband's business partner, unease gripping her stomach. "What did you learn, Frank?"

"Last night I saw Eloise's father for the first time since the funeral. He told me that when Eloise died, Daniel inherited money her grandmother left her." Frank sighed and took Katie's hands in his, staring into her eyes. "The vineyard was out of money. He had no money left."

Nausea rose in Katie, her stomach clenching with the need to lose the contents of her stomach. Why hadn't Daniel told her about Eloise. They had yet to have a discussion about his wife, where he told his side of the story. And she desperately needed to hear from her husband.

Pulling her hands from his, she stood and began to walk around the room. "So you think he killed her for her money?"

Frank rose and came to her side. "What else? He loves this vineyard. It's been his dream since he learned about Thomas Jefferson's attempt to make wine at his beloved Monticello. Daniel needed that money to help him hang onto his dream."

For a moment, Katie felt skeptical. This didn't make sense. The man she'd fallen in love with would never be this diabolical. He wouldn't kill his wife to take her inheritance. "So why would he bring you in as a partner if he already had the funds?"

Frank laughed. "It's brilliant. Because this way the town didn't know he needed her money. How would it appear to people if they learned, his wife died of exposure, his vineyard was broke, but now suddenly he received an influx of cash from his dead wife's estate?" He paused, nodding his head. "Don't you see it's all coming together. Daniel killed Eloise to save the vineyard."

Katie frowned. What he was saying made logical sense, but her heart refused to believe what he was divulging. Her body and soul didn't believe Daniel could hurt anyone in order to save his vineyard.

"For your safety, you should come with me," Frank said pacing the floor. "At least until the sheriff investigates and we learn the truth, you'll be safe."

There was no way she was leaving with Frank. Daniel would never forgive her, if she went with him and she wasn't convinced Frank's story was real. Her instincts were telling her Daniel was innocent and she didn't know what Frank was doing, but this couldn't be good.

"No. I don't believe Daniel killed Eloise. It may appear from what you're saying that he did, but in my heart, I know he wouldn't harm her. He told me he loved her and I believe him."

"Please come with me. You're in danger. I'm trying to save your life."

Something wasn't right. Her husband was not a killer. Images of the factory fire and how they'd all run for their lives to escape the flames came to mind. Bob Brown was a killer. He'd deliberately set the place on fire while his workers were inside. Daniel was not a cruel man like Mr. Brown. Daniel did not kill Eloise.

"I appreciate you driving out here to express your concerns, but I'm not worried."

Frank's emerald eyes flashed with anger. "When he hurts you, I'm not responsible."

"You're right. You're not."

She walked to the door. "Thanks for coming by, Frank."

The man huffed out the door while she watched him leave. Was she crazy for not going with him? Only time would tell.

~

Later that evening, Daniel watched his wife who sat on the loveseat, working on a piece of needlepoint. He loved to gaze at her as she concentrated on her pulling the needle and thread through the canvas.

His life was so much better this last month since she'd come into his house and made it into a home. Even his mother was happier and seemed to be getting around better. And her disposition was such an improvement.

But who could remain unhappy around his smiling, warm wife. The room brightened when she stepped in with her smile and laughter. She was like a breath of fresh air and sunshine swirling through the room, leaving it a better place.

No, he hadn't ordered a mail-order bride, but thank God, Frank had seen his need and placed the ad that brought Katie to him.

She glanced at him. Tonight, he could sense something was bothering her and whatever it was, he wanted to fix it and bring back the bubbly girl that made him smile.

"What?" she asked, staring at him.

"I'm just enjoying watching you," he said. And he was. Quickly he'd learned that Katie was excellent with needlepoint, sewing, and decorating cookies. She would be an excellent mother to his children and in so many ways he'd been blessed with her arrival.

Her eyes looked away and he knew she was troubled. "What's wrong?"

Putting the canvas down, she gazed at him, her emerald eyes darkening. "When are you going to tell me about Eloise? I haven't heard your side, but everyone has given me their version of how she died. People have told me you killed her. And when you won't talk about that night, I begin to have doubts. You should trust me enough to talk to me about what happened, and you don't."

Sorrow gripped him, squeezing his chest at the thought she would believe he killed his first wife. At the idea anyone thought him capable of murder.

He wanted to run away from the ugliness, his muscles unable to sit any longer. Rising from the chair he moved closer to the fire, hoping it would warm the ice flowing through his veins.

"I'd been working late every night the week she died. It had been a brutal winter and I'd had the crew out at night watering the vines, keeping the fires burning in the fields, to keep the vines from freezing.

"Eloise had been distant. She'd not shared my bed since October and the worst part was I didn't know what I'd done. Trying to keep her happy, I gave into most of her demands.

She didn't like living outside of town. She hated that my mother lived with us. And she wanted me to go to work for her father in Raleigh."

He paused, remembering that awful night. The way his wife had laughed when she told him about the affair. The pain of her betrayal gripped his insides. "When I came in from the fields, for the first time in months, she was waiting for me. Told me she had found someone else. Someone who would treat her the way she deserved to be treated. Someone who would give her the life she wanted. Said she was leaving in the morning."

"What did you do?"

Laughing he looked at the woman he knew he was falling in love with. Katie listened to him, worked with him, and made him look good. Yet he couldn't give her his complete trust. The differences between the two women were suddenly so clear.

"At first, I tried to talk her into staying. I wanted to work things out, but she wanted no part of any reconciliation. The realization that my marriage was over slammed into me like a boulder. I'd loved Eloise deeply. But her mind was made up and I wasn't going to change it."

And here was where everything became fuzzy. He'd slept hard that night. He'd been exhausted and after their argument had several glasses of wine. He'd not been drunk when he went to sleep, but he'd had enough wine that he slept well that night.

"When I left, Eloise, she was retiring for bed. Mother called me into her room and poured me a cup of tea. I didn't mention that Eloise was leaving in the morning. We talked about the wine and then I went upstairs to bed. I was so tired and as soon as my head hit the pillow I was asleep. The next morning when I woke up, she was gone."

Daniel remembered the feeling of knocking on her bedroom door, and when she didn't answer, opening to see the empty room, the bed that had not been slept in. Her suitcase open like she hadn't finished packing.

"Did you try to find her."

"Of course, I did. I was the one who searched the woods. Who found her cold body half buried in the snow," his voice choked. "There was blood on the snow from a gash on the back of her head. But the weirdest thing was she had no coat on, no shoes." He shivered at the memory. "No one should die like that."

He walked to the window and stared out at the falling flakes, remembering the horror of finding her dead. "I'd give anything to find out what happened and why she went out that night."

"Do you still love her?" Katie asked, her voice soft and mild.

No, he no longer loved Eloise. He was falling for Katie, but he didn't want to tell her while they were talking about his dead wife. Turning, he faced Katie. "No. Our marriage had never been a happy one and when she said she was leaving, I actually felt relief."

At first he'd been upset, but then he realized how he could never have made her happy and it was probably for the best she left. This way another man could try to give her what she wanted in life.

"Did you kill her?"

His head jerked, feeling like he'd been slapped, her words stung. "Never."

"But you want to know who did?"

"Of course. Not only to clear my name, but so I would know who had done this to Eloise. She deserves justice."

He gazed at the woman he was rapidly falling for. She had been so trusting, believing in him, and he'd avoided telling her his side of the story. He'd been wrong and didn't know how to make it up to her. Last night had been the best night of his life and somehow he wanted to hold onto what they'd had together.

"Come to bed, Katie," he said softly.

She glanced away, her face tightened as she bit her bottom lip. Did she not believe him? Daniel felt his heart wrench inside his chest like someone had punched him. He should have told her the first night she arrived, before she was influenced by other people's version of the truth. But he'd been trying to put the past behind him.

"I need some time. I'll be up soon, but right now I just want to sit here and think for a few moments."

His stomach tightened, nausea rising. "This is why I hadn't told you. I didn't want you to believe I'd killed her."

She said she didn't believe he'd killed Eloise, but still there was something holding her back.

She sighed. "I don't think you killed her. I just need some time to consider what you've told me. I learned about Eloise from everyone else until tonight. Tonight I finally hear your side. Is this a sign of you finally trusting me?"

"I do trust you," he said.

"Then why whenever something happens in the vineyard do you believe it's me?"

"Before you arrived, I wasn't having any problems and now suddenly every time I turn around something has gone wrong. What am I supposed to think?" he said, having a hard time believing his sweet wife would create havoc in his vineyard, but then he would think back to how his first wife had acted and he feared Katie was doing the same. He felt torn.

"Did you ever consider that maybe someone wants you to think it's me." She sighed and hung her head. "I'm not Eloise, Daniel, and I refuse to battle her ghost."

It wasn't fair to compare her to Eloise. He knew it and he was trying, but he'd been burned before. "I'm doing my best, Katie. Really I am. But Eloise betrayed me and I fear you will too."

~

Katie watched her husband climb the stairs, his retreating back so strong and muscular. Had she fallen in love with a murderer? No, there was no way Daniel would have harmed Eloise.

Her husband was an honest, hard-working soul, but never a murderer. But what could have sent the woman fleeing into the snow?

The only people in the house were Daniel and his wheelchair ridden mother. Neither seemed capable of forcing Eloise into the cold. Unless it was the lover his mother claimed Eloise had.

But who could that be? And did they work here in the vineyard?

So many questions swirling around in her head and she truly did not know who to believe.

Tears sprang to her eyes. Daniel expected her to trust him when he said he hadn't killed Eloise, but he couldn't trust her when it came to the accidents in the vineyard. Sitting in the parlor she let the tears slide down her cheeks. Pain clenched her chest. The very idea that the man she loved thought she could harm their crops or destroy their wine, broke her heart.

Tomorrow the ladies from the church would be attending a tea party she was putting on and she would have to face them knowing they suspected her husband of murder and he believed she was causing damage to the vineyard.

Had the journey from Lawrenceville been worth the heartache she'd found here in Charlottesville?

Chapter Ten

Daniel was late this morning. He'd overslept after not being able to rest peacefully most of the night. Katie had not come to bed until late. He'd missed the feel of holding her in his arms and this morning she was busy preparing for her tea. Neither one of them had slept well.

"Before you leave for the fields, would you bring up a couple of bottles from the wine cellar?" she asked.

He really didn't have time, but he wasn't about to deny her any small request at this point. Hurrying down the cellar stairs, the smell of alcohol stunned him. When he reached the bottom he stared in shock, his chest aching with pain.

Broken bottles were strewn about like a cyclone had lifted them and smashed them against the floor. At least two cases of his best wine was evaporating on the ground. How could this have happened without anyone noticing the noise?

After hearing his story last night had she gotten her revenge by shattering his best wine?

Since her arrival someone had been doing their best to try to destroy the vineyard, but why? And why would Katie harm the very livelihood that kept her off the streets? It didn't make sense. Nothing was making sense these days and somehow he had to learn who was behind this. It had to stop, now.

If it was Katie...his chest tightened and his head began to throb. Had he once again chosen a woman who wanted to destroy him?

Sinking down on his heels, he touched the wine littered floor. It had been here for a day or two as it was already evaporating.

Fortunately, the destruction was either a warning or they'd been interrupted in their attempt to demolish the wine in the cellar. They'd only gotten to two cases, but still it was enough to frighten him.

Grabbing two bottles, he hurried up the stairs. Katie was sliding what looked like a coffee cake into the oven.

She turned and smiled at him, in that way that chased the dark thoughts from his heart and brightened his day. There was no way she could be behind this devastation.

"Thank you. I have your breakfast almost ready," she said.

When he didn't move, her facial expression drained like an hourglass. "What's wrong?"

He wanted to see if she was lying. "Someone broke several cases of wine in the cellar."

"Oh no," she said. "Why is this happening?"

"If I knew the answer to that, the mystery would be solved. When was the last time you were down in the cellar?"

She frowned. "The night of the party, Why?"

"I just wanted to know."

She bit her lip, her eyes darkening. "I forgot to tell you, but the night of the party, Martha found several shattered bottles. When I came in to take the glasses to our guests there was wine and glass strewn across the kitchen. I even checked people's clothes for wine stains, but nothing.

"I didn't tell you right then because I didn't want to spoil the party for you. Then afterwards you and Frank were in that heated discussion and after that I learned you hadn't sent for me. And I forgot."

The fact she hadn't told him left him leery. They were under attack. How could he fight if he didn't know when to battle? Unless of course the enemy had infiltrated the base. Anger churned through him and he took a deep breath. "You should have told me."

"I meant to, but things were a little hectic at the time."

"I'm going to have one of the men come over and put a lock on the cellar. No one is to go in or out without me here, do you understand?"

"Of course." Her brow drew together in a frown. "Daniel O'Malley, you don't think I did this, do you?"

"I don't know what to think. This all started when you arrived. But that doesn't mean you're the one behind this."

As soon as he said the words, he knew he should have kept his suspicions to himself.

She whirled back to the stove, dished up his eggs and laid the plate down on the table.

"Enjoy, I need to make certain everything is ready for my tea." And walked out of the room.

Whatever progress they'd had made as a couple was looking bleaker by the minute.

$\sim$

Two hours later, Katie was still indignant over her husband's lack of trust and suspicions. She'd been trying all morning to put her hurt feelings aside, but it was hard. The man she loved, who she admired and felt grateful for, thought she was trying to destroy him and his precious grapes.

It took a lot to make Katie mad, but right now not only had his accusations hurt, they'd left her disillusioned and questioning why she was here. Marriage was built on trust and Daniel obviously thought the worst of her.

Yet she didn't believe he'd killed his wife. She trusted him more than he trusted her and that made her even angrier.

Katie's lips felt frozen in a permanent grin as she mingled among her guest from church, doing her best to keep a smile on and pretend everything was fine.

But her heart ached with the knowledge he thought she was damaging his vineyard. And why she thought inviting these women would help with the suspicion over Daniel was enough for a good laugh. They were here snooping.

Shaking her head, she closed her eyes, hoping this would soon be over. Why in the world would she try to destroy the new life she loved? Why would she hurt the man who had married her and taken her into his home? And why didn't he realize she loved him?

"Katie, dear, where did you come from?" the old biddy in the group asked. Katie called her an old biddy because frankly she'd watched her stirring up trouble the entire time she was here.

"I worked in Lawrenceville, Massachusetts until a factory fire claimed my job."

"You worked?"

"Yes, ma'am."

"Well, I must say you've done an amazing job on this house. Eloise, God rest her soul, she just didn't have the touch," a dark-haired elderly woman said.

Katie smiled. She knew they'd come on a fishing expedition to try to learn what she knew about Eloise's death. Well, she refused to answer their curiosity. "Thank you."

"You do know about Eloise," another woman asked lifting her tea cup.

"Yes, I do. What I would love to know about Eloise is who was her lover? That way we could finally solve her murder and my husband's name would be cleared," Katie replied anger roaring in her ears like a tiger on the prowl. As she stared at the shocked faces around her, she couldn't help but feel a smidgeon of pleasure. She smiled. "Is everyone ready for Christmas?"

Somehow she had to steer them away from the topic of Eloise and back to safe tea discussions. Or she could lose her temper completely and send them all running for the door.

"We need to decorate a tree and that's it," one woman said. "Don't you just love the smell of pine in the house."

The door to the house burst open and Daniel strode in looking like a madman. His dark hair was windblown, his face twisted with anger. "Katie, why?"

She rose from her seat in a chair and faced him, her heart beating rapidly at the sight of her husband. "What's wrong?"

"Jack said you were walking in the vines this morning. Why are you trying to ruin me?"

Confused, she stared at him. He had the nerve to come in here and accuse her in front of her guests?

"Yes, I went for a walk in the vineyard to cool off after you accused me of shattering two cases of wine. But I have no clue as to what you are referring to. What's happened?"

"You're the only person who has been in that section of the vineyard. It has to be you."

"Tell me what I've done?" she said her voice raising. She was so tired of him thinking she was the one causing the problems in his vineyard. This had to stop or it was going to end their marriage.

"You poured kerosene on the vines and then lit them."

She paused staring at him like she didn't know who he was. He came in here and accused her of trying to set the vineyard on fire, while they had guests. While women from their church were here in their home attending a tea, he had the nerve to confront her.

"Mr. O'Malley, if I knew where you kept the kerosene, I might be tempted to light a fire under you to leave my tea party. But I have no idea where you keep the liquid. Have you ever considered that one of your hands is possibly doing the damage? I would suggest you begin looking there."

"But you've been near every single accident."

"That doesn't mean I'm the person responsible for the sabotage. Someone is trying to make it look like me."

Shaking his head, he stood there, face flushed, hands on his hips. "This didn't start until you arrived."

"Why would I damage our livelihood? Don't you think I understand what it's like when the business you work for fails?"

"Maybe you were the one who started that fire?"

Katie felt like he'd slapped her. She could have died the day the factory burned. She'd been running out of the building with the rest of the women, frantically searching for her friends. His comment was such an insult. Tears sprang to her eyes.

"That comment, sir, does not deserve a response."

The women from church were all staring at the two of them in shock and Katie had never been more embarrassed in her life. Humiliation flowed through her veins almost strangling her.

Daniel clenched his fists. "I've worked so hard. Why do you want to put an end to what I've built? I'm so angry right now, I don't think I can look at you another minute."

"Then leave. You've disrupted my tea quite enough," she said, her heart breaking, wondering how they could go on after this.

Like he had forgotten they were there, he suddenly glanced around the room at the women from church. "Excuse me, ladies."

He strode from the room.

"I'm so sorry, Katie, I really need to be going," the older woman said standing and searching the room for her reticule.

"Me too. It was...charming," someone else said.

Katie felt numb. The man she loved had made her look like the biggest laughing stock in town. She knew for a fact the women would hurry home to their husbands and tell them what they'd witnessed. How could she ever hold her head up in church again?

One by one, they all said their goodbyes leaving Katie to an empty house that seemed to echo with empty promises.

Sinking down into the chair, she stared at the teapot, the glasses and the cookies she'd made for the event. A surge of anger rushed from her head to her toes, bringing tears to her eyes.

His mother rolled her wheelchair into the living room. She was silent for a moment. "I'm going to my room to rest for a while."

Katie didn't respond. She couldn't without breaking down into tears.

She loved Daniel, she wanted to be his wife, but he believed she was trying to destroy his vineyard and their livelihood, which for the life of her she didn't understand. If they failed how would they make a living?

She didn't believe the worst about him, but he thought she'd deliberately harm his business. A good marriage could not exist without trust. And she wasn't willing to watch the man she loved decimate them until she hated him.

Maybe when she left, he'd see it wasn't her causing the damage to the vineyard. It was someone he'd obviously overlooked.

She'd go back to Lawrenceville, meet up with Julia and together maybe the two of them could find jobs. She'd given marriage a try. She'd even fallen in love with Daniel, but how could she live with him when he didn't trust her and believed she would harm him.

Heart weary, tears ran down her cheeks, she went upstairs to pack. She would catch the next train to Lawrenceville even if that meant she had to spend the night in town.

~

Daniel strode out of the house feeling like the biggest fool. If his wife ever forgave him, it would be a miracle. He'd acted irrationally. From the look on Katie's face, he knew she'd not poured kerosene on his youngest vines, damaging them permanently. It had to be one of his workers and he had to find out who.

Then he would return and grovel at his wife's feet to forgive him.

He watched as Martha walked towards the house. "Good morning, Mr. O'Malley."

"Good morning," he said, stepping in front of her. Her eyes widened and she stopped. "Katie told me you found broken wine bottles in the kitchen the night of the party. Do you have any idea what happened."

The woman's skin flushed and she licked her lips nervously. "Yes, when I walked back into the kitchen they were broken."

Why was she out of the kitchen? She'd left them in a vulnerable position and he couldn't stand for it any longer.

"But you were supposed to stay in the kitchen that night and make certain the food trays were ready and the drinks were ready," he said. "So how could someone sneak into the kitchen."

Her eyes grew wide, her pupils dilating. "A lady does have to use the outhouse occasionally."

Daniel shook his head. "No. You know who broke those bottles. And I bet you know who broke the two cases in the cellar."

"Mr. O'Malley, I like my job. I don't want to lose it. I would never do anything to cause me to get fired."

He took a deep breath. "I understand. But you see, I'm thinking about firing every person working for me right

                    Sylvia McDaniel

now. Because I think someone is trying to ruin the vineyard and maybe even send me to prison for murder.

"So if I fire everyone, I think I'll take care of the person who is causing the trouble. Someone has to know what's going on and why. And I'm not willing to take any more chances. So effective immediately, everyone is fired. You're the first one to know."

The older woman's eyes widened. "No, you can't do that. My husband works for you and I work for you. We've lived here for thirty years."

"I'm sorry, then someone better start talking."

Daniel started to walk off, when she reached out and grabbed him by the arm. "Yes?"

"It's Jack Edwards, your foreman. He broke the bottles in the kitchen and in the cellar. He broke those bottles with a hammer and a cloth over them to soften the noise and keep wine from getting wine on him. He told me to keep my mouth shut or he'd make certain we were both fired. Talk to my husband. He can tell you about what's been happening in the fields."

"Why didn't you come forward and tell me before now? Are you so afraid of me that you don't think you can talk to me about what's happening?" Daniel asked.

Martha sighed. "No, sir, but he told me he would make certain that my grandson went to jail for the murder of your wife, if I said anything. I love my grandson and I feared with no one being accused and him being a young black man, he could find some way to pin her killing on Thomas. I love that boy."

Daniel could understand her fear. While the Civil War was long over, the tension between the races still ran high. And he would hate to see someone wrongly accused.

"Thank you, Martha. I understand. If I could find out who Eloise's killer was, I would put that behind us as well."

The older woman bit her lip and hung her head. "Sir, the day before she died, she came back from town happy. She asked me to go to the cellar and bring her, her suitcase, said she would soon be leaving. I didn't question her, because I knew she went to see her father several times a year. When I came back up the cellar steps, she was at the back door having a heated conversation with someone."

"Did you hear what they were saying?"

It was the first new clue he'd had in over a year.

"All I heard was her saying, I'll see you tonight."

Daniel leaned his head back, thinking he was so close to learning the truth. "But you didn't see a face?"

She shook her head. "And I didn't hear the man's voice."

"So someone came to the kitchen door and arranged to meet Eloise that night."

"Yes, sir," she said.

"What time of day was it?"

"Probably around three o'clock," she said, gazing at him worriedly. "Oh, there was one other thing. When Eloise shut the door, she laughed and said he isn't getting a dime."

Daniel shook his head. "Why didn't you tell me this after Eloise died? Why didn't you tell the sheriff?"

She sighed. "I wanted to, but I'm an old black woman and no one would have believed me."

He laughed. "I understand that completely. No one believes me either."

Leaning his head in his hand, he stared at the woman who had worked for him for years. "I think it's time I paid a visit to Jack and just see what he says. Somehow I've got to figure out if he's the one who's been destroying the vineyard."

And then he had to apologize to Katie. He'd been cruel to the woman he loved and that wasn't right.

The older woman stood. "Do I have a job?"

"Of course. If my workers would talk to me, I bet we could find out who was behind these incidents and send them on their way."

"Can I go now? I need to get to the house before it looks suspicious and he comes after me."

"Does he make all of my employees fear him?" Daniel asked.

She smiled. "Yes."

Nodding, Daniel said, "Thanks, Martha. Please never hesitate to come talk to me if there's a problem."

"Thank you, sir."

The older woman hurried out of the barn, while Daniel sat at the table trying to figure out his next move.

~

Daniel had hired Jack Edwards because Frank had referred him. Said he came with excellent references. Now he was questioning those references and wondering why the man was out to ruin him. Eventually, he would talk to all of his employees, but right now he wanted to start with his foreman.

Walking to Jack's house, he glanced around at the cottage that had come with the property. Two smaller cottages were occupied by Martha and her family and then the third was filled with single men. Normally, he avoided the area not wanting his workers to think he was spying on them and to give them some hours away from the business.

He walked up the stairs and knocked. Jack came to the door. "Good day, sir. I was just eating lunch."

"Can I come in?"

"Of course," he said opening the wooden door.

Daniel walked into the small house and glanced around at the scattered clothes and dishes. The man wasn't much for cleaning.

"Have a seat," Jack said pointing to a saggy sofa. "What can I do for you?"

Taking a seat, Daniel glanced around at the room, there were three pieces of furniture and nothing else, no pictures, nothing. "I wanted to talk to you about this morning's attempt to burn us out."

"Yes, we got lucky," Jack said shaking his head. "The vines were wet enough that the kerosene didn't burn, though the plants are probably ruined."

"How many do you think we lost?"

"It looks like at least one row, if not two, from what I can tell," he said.

The room felt chilly in the early morning air and Daniel shivered.

"Oh, let me throw another log on the fire. It stays chilly in here unless I'm burning word," Jack said, rising and putting another log into the rock fireplace.

Daniel stared at the hearth, there was a stone missing. The previous owners had told him of how they hauled big river rocks from the Rivanna River to decorate not only the big house, but the cottages on the property. They were unique smooth – silver stones that were excellent for decoration. And Jack had one missing from his hearth.

Eloise had died from her head hitting a big stone like the one missing from Jack's hearth. They didn't think the fall killed her, but rather the cold, she'd been unconscious and unable to return to the house.

Anger surged through Daniel like a dam breaking. He wanted to pound the man, but he couldn't. He had to first prove Jack was the killer and then let the sheriff arrest him or his name would never be cleared.

But part of him just wanted to beat the man into a senseless bloody pulp. He took a deep breath and cleared his throat.

Jack turned back from the fireplace and stared at Daniel.

"What's our next move to protect the vineyard?"

"I thought tonight we would set up patrols. No one goes near the vines. Two men patrolling all the time," Daniel said.

Nodding in agreement, Jack smiled. "I'll get some volunteers or assign someone and we'll get on it. Is there anything else, boss?"

Oh there was so much more. Like why was he trying to destroy the vineyard, but most of all why had he killed Eloise?

"No, I've got to run into town for a bit. Just make certain the vineyard is protected all the time," Daniel said.

"Will do."

Daniel stood and walked to the door. He had to get out of here. He didn't know why, but he felt like Eloise had died here in this cottage. He had to get the law.

Knowing he was being watched, Daniel strolled towards the barn and his horse, when all he wanted to do was run. When he got to the barn, Martha's husband was frowning, waiting for him.

"George, I need you to watch the house and not let the ladies alone with Jack while I go to town. Can you do that?"

"Yes, sir. My wife said she spoke to you."

"Yes, and she's a good woman. Now watch the place well and I'll be back as soon as I can. And this stays between us."

"Yes, sir."

Still trying to appear like nothing was urgent, Daniel rode his horse out of the yard, praying he wasn't making a mistake going off and leaving the women and the vineyards in Jack's destructive hands.

Chapter Eleven

It was a wonder, Daniel didn't kill his horse as he rode hell-bent to Charlottesville to the sheriff's office. And then it had seemed to take forever to convince the sheriff to talk to Jack.

He knew he was taking a risk on the man running, if he didn't confess, but Daniel had the rock that had killed Eloise. A rock that for some reason he'd laid on her grave. He didn't know why, but the stone was stained with her blood and he didn't want a reminder of her death lying on his land. So he'd taken the rock and placed it on her grave.

The sheriff had seen the rock and while he thought Daniel's idea was a little far-fetched, he agreed to follow him back to the vineyard.

As they rode up to the house, Daniel felt relief to see everything appeared normal.

"Mr. Edwards's cottage is down here," Daniel said.

At the hitching post they both climbed down. The sheriff walked up the steps and knocked on the door.

Daniel followed a few steps behind, his fists clenching, his stomach churning. Jack came to the door, a frown drawing together between his eyes at the sheriff.

"Good afternoon, Mr. Edwards. Could we come in and talk for a spell."

"I'm on my way out. I'm needed in the vineyard," he said, taking a step out the door. It was then that he saw Daniel and frowned.

"Whatever you're needed for in the vineyard, can wait," Daniel said, trying not to let the anger reflect in his voice and show nothing but calmness.

The man's face blanched and he took a step back. "Why certainly, come in, gentlemen."

The sheriff carried the rock in his hand. "I see you're missing a stone from your hearth."

"Yes, it came out a couple of years ago and was never replaced."

Daniel knew that was a lie. "You've only been my foreman for the last twenty months."

"Two years, twenty months, it's all the same," the man said with a shrug, his hands shaking.

The sheriff glanced at him. "Do you mind if I see if this is the missing stone?"

"Yes, I do. Where did that stone come from?" Jack asked getting excited.

For over a year, Daniel had been accused of being Eloise's murderer and he'd taken the abuse at the hands of Charlottesville citizens, but no more. "It's the rock that killed Eloise. It came from her grave."

"Well, it won't fit in my fireplace," Jack said moving nervously. "I didn't have anything to do with her killing."

"No one said you did," the sheriff said as he walked over to the hearth and placed the rock in the empty space. It fit perfectly. It was the missing stone that had been there to begin with.

Slowly, the sheriff stood. "Why did you kill her?"

"I didn't kill her...I..."

"You're the one who has been destroying the vineyard. Martha told me about you breaking the bottles of wine, the other men are now coming forward and telling me what you've done. Why, Jack? Why did you kill Eloise?" Daniel asked advancing toward the man.

The sheriff stepped between them and took out his handcuffs. "You're going to jail for an awfully long time. Why did you kill her?"

"It was an accident. She came over here and she fell and hit her head on the stone. I didn't kill her."

The man's eyes were wide with fright and Daniel knew finally he was learning the truth about Eloise's death. "Why was she here? Were you blackmailing her?"

He drew his lips together, his face scrunching. "It wasn't blackmail. I wanted money to keep quiet about her having an affair with your friend Frank."

The world seemed to tilt suddenly and Daniel couldn't believe what he was hearing from this man. "What?"

"I saw the two of them together. I told her if she didn't pay me, I was going to tell you. When she came over here, she said you knew she was leaving and she wasn't paying me a dime. When she got up to leave, she fell."

Yes, he'd known she was leaving him for another man, but he had no idea who that man was. His chest seized with a burning sensation like nothing he'd ever felt before.

He couldn't breathe as the realization that his best friend, his college roommate, had betrayed him with his wife. She'd been expecting Frank's baby, not his.

And after her death, Frank still remained and acted like his friend. But why?

"The only way, she could have that kind of injury on the back of her head from a fall was if someone pushed her. You pushed her, didn't you," the sheriff asked.

"But I didn't mean for her to fall and hit her head on the hearth. I just wanted her to pay me what I demanded and she refused."

"What if she wasn't dead when you took her out there? What if she was just knocked out?" Daniel cried.

"Oh, she was dead, all right. I made sure. But I took her shoes and coat to make it appear that she ran."

"You bastard, she was pregnant," Daniel said. "She was expecting a baby."

Jack looked up at him. "I only wanted more money, which your good friend, her lover is now paying me to destroy your vineyard."

Daniel swung at the man and the sheriff stepped between, blocking his punch. "Mr. O'Malley, I think it would be best if you waited outside."

"Hell, no. I want to see you arrest him for the murder of Eloise," Daniel said. "For eighteen months I've been accused of her death, when I was innocent. I deserve to hear those words. I also want to press charges against him and Frank for the destruction of property."

The sheriff nodded in understanding. "Jack Edwards, you're under the arrest for the murder of Eloise O'Malley and destruction of property."

He slapped the hand cuffs on Jack and clicked them shut. "Let's get him back to town."

Daniel walked outside and waved down one of his hands. "Bring me the wagon."

A few minutes later, the wagon pulled up in front of the cottage and the hands who had gathered around watched as the sheriff led Jack out in handcuffs. Daniel helped load him into the wagon.

"Sheriff, I have to talk to my wife and then I'll meet you in town and we can confront Frank. Give me an hour and I'll be there. I'd like to hear what he has to say when you arrest him."

"Will do. I'll meet you back in town."

As the sun sank in the sky, the wagon pulled away, and the hands clapped and cheered as Jack was taken to jail. Daniel couldn't help but smile as it felt like a rock had been lifted from his shoulders. He glanced at the cottage and wished Eloise's spirit to rest well. Her murderer would soon be sitting behind bars.

Now he had to apologize profusely to the love of his life, his Katie.

$\sim$

Katie drove the buggy to the train station intent on returning to Lawrenceville as soon as possible. She had to get away from Daniel, not because she didn't love him, but because she feared he would convince her to stay even though he didn't trust her.

And she couldn't. Having to face him every day while he believed she was the one causing the vineyard harm would eventually tear her apart.

Pulling on the reins she parked the buggy in front of the train station where she'd buy her ticket, knowing she would have to wait, but at least she was here. Daniel would find his horse and carriage and realize she was gone.

Staring at the building, she remembered how she'd gotten off that train so full of hope and determined to make a new life for herself. She'd been frightened and filled with joy at the same time.

And when she saw Daniel standing there beside Frank, she'd known he was the one. There was something about her husband that drew her to him and yet he hadn't been the one to order a mail-order bride. Frank had been corresponding as Daniel.

But why would he send a bride to his friend? And why would he try to turn her against Daniel? Nothing made sense.

Slowly her mind played the last few weeks of her life with Daniel. The dinner where Daniel became upset with Frank for talking to that tobacco company and wanting to sell the land to them. The party, where she suddenly remembered seeing Frank walking down the hall moments before she went into the kitchen and found a distraught Martha.

He could have gone down to the wine cellar and done the exact same thing during the party and they hadn't found it until this morning. There was the cattle incident and the kerosene in the vineyard this morning. Someone was definitely trying to ruin Daniel, but it wasn't her.

Who could it be? And what was their reason for hurting her husband?

She glanced down the street and saw Frank's office building not far. What if Frank was the one destroying the crops?

Jumping from the buggy, she tied the reins of the horse to the hitching post and hurried down the street. She was going to do a little snooping. She might find nothing, but then again, she might find what she needed to know.

The office lights were dim. It looked to be closed. Turning the knob, she opened the door and stepped inside, surprised at the unlocked door. Glancing around, she wondered which office was Frank's.

Stepping quietly to the back, she walked to an office door, and peeked in, but it wasn't Frank's. Hurrying past two more doors she found an office with a plague that read Frank Lowe. Stepping into the room, she quickly lit a gas lamp.

She had no idea what she was searching for, but somehow she hoped something would show her where Frank's loyalties lay. Was he a true partner and her husband's best friend or not. She just needed a sign.

Crossing to his desk, she rifled through the papers on his desk. None of it made sense, but she glanced at each page and then hurried on to the next.

Sinking into his chair, she began to flip among files in a filing cabinet off to the side. She came across a label named Southern Virginia Tobacco and Land Company. Wasn't that the name he'd mentioned coming to visit the vineyard? Opening the folder, she saw a contract for Daniel's land. All that was needed was Daniel's signature.

"You know I wanted to bring you to town yesterday, but you refused."

Her heart skipped a beat and she tried to hide the folder in her skirts. She smiled at Frank standing in the doorway, watching her. She tried her best to hide the fear spreading through her faster than quicksand. He had a contract on the land. Why?

"Then tonight I was eating supper in the restaurant and happened to hear this woman talking about your tea this afternoon. She said that Daniel acted horrid to you and she didn't know why you put up with him. And now here you are."

Nonchalantly she moved paperwork around on his desk including the letter opener. "Yes, here I am." She shrugged. "We had a disagreement."

"He thinks you're trying to destroy the vineyard." He laughed. "You're such a naughty girl."

Frank glanced at the filing cabinet, she was certain to see how far she'd gotten in the files. Why would he say such a thing to her when she knew she was not the one doing the damage. Could it be Frank?

"But I'm not the one who is harming the crops," she said bewildered. She yanked up the contract and held it before him. "What's this, Frank? Why do you have a signed contract on the land."

He shut his office door and a chill went down Katie's spine. She was in his office and no one knew she was here. She swallowed the fear roaring inside.

"The contract." Frank sighed. "I could double what Daniel paid for that land. But he refuses to even consider selling." He shrugged. "But you've solved the problem."

She frowned. "What are you talking about? I would never help you sell his land."

If he thought she would help him, harm her husband, he was crazy. She was desperately trying to find a way to leave without him stopping her. He stood between her and the door or she would have run out.

"Dear, the moment you agreed to marry him, you were helping me. You see, Daniel is suspected of killing his first wife. When his second wife is found dead after a big argument witnessed by several ladies from church, well, people will know he killed you."

Katie felt her heart beating rapidly in her chest. He'd been setting this up all along. He hadn't been looking out for Daniel, he'd been planning on sending him to prison so he could sell the vineyard.

"But Daniel would never harm me."

She watched in horror as Frank pulled a gun from his waistband and pointed the weapon at her. "Maybe not, but I have no qualms about shooting you and then planting the gun on Daniel. He'll never suspect and then when they find your body and the gun on his property, he'll hang for your murder."

Everything was falling into place for Frank and she knew it. Somehow she had to find a way ruin his plan – to save Daniel and herself.

"Frank, why would you do this? You're his best friend. Do you need the money from the land that badly?"

His eyes darkened and she could see the determination in his face. Anger seemed to radiate from him. "It's not the money. He let the woman I love die. I loved Eloise. She was leaving him for me. He threw her out in the cold and she died." His voice caught. "She was having my child."

Now it all made sense. Frank was Eloise's lover. But it wasn't Daniel who had pushed Eloise in the cold.

"You're wrong. Daniel didn't kill Eloise. Don't do this, Frank. You're a better man," she said trying to appeal to his better side, if he had one. He'd been friends with her husband for a long time. "You know my husband. He would never kill anyone."

He yanked a chair into the middle of the room. "Shut up. Come, sit in this chair. When midnight arrives, I'll take you out into the cold and shoot you on Daniel's property. Just like Eloise was killed on his property."

Katie feared once he tied her up, she would never get loose. She would die.

"No. I'm not going to make this easy. In fact, I'll fight you every step of the way."

Walking over to her, he grabbed her by the arm and yanked her towards him. He was too strong. She raised the letter opener she'd hidden in the folds of her skirt and aimed her slash at his neck. He jerked away and the letter opener sank into his shoulder, the steel point sinking deeply into his flesh.

A scream ripped from his throat as he kicked her, knocking her to the floor. She landed on her back, air swooshing from her lungs. Dazed she lay there, disappointment surging through her that she'd missed his neck. Pointing the gun at her, he screamed, "Get in the chair or I'll shoot you right now."

Slowly she rose from the floor. "Frank, stop you'll never get away with this."

"Shut up. Yes, I will."

"Daniel will come after me. He'll find me and he'll kill you."

For some reason, she suddenly knew the words were true. She'd made a mistake leaving him and not fighting to help him realize she wasn't the one doing the damage. She should have stayed and fought for the vineyard, for Daniel.

~

Elated with the news of learning who had killed Eloise, and attempting to destroy the vineyard, Daniel hurried into the house, knowing he owed his wife an apology. When he opened the door, silence greeted him.

No lights were burning, no smells coming from the kitchen, no laughter or even the sound of Katie walking about. Hurrying into the parlor, he saw the tea pot and cookies still sitting where they'd been earlier this morning.

A heavy quietness hung over the house and his heart clenched in pain.

He'd let his temper get the better of him and acted like a fool in front of the ladies from church. He knew he'd embarrassed Katie and she'd done nothing wrong. He'd let his fears from the past overwhelm his good judgement and possibly ruin his chance at happiness.

Hurrying up the stairs, he threw open their bedroom door. The bed was made, the room tidy, everything looked the same. Pulling open the armoire he saw her clothes were gone. He yanked open her drawers in the dresser, empty. Her tattered carpetbag was gone.

Defeated he trudged down the stairs. Katie had been a light that brightened his home, his life, his very existence, and he'd made a huge mistake in accusing her of damaging the vineyard.

She'd done nothing but try to make his home and his life a happier place, while he accused her of wrong doing. Just like people blamed him for Eloise's death.

Walking into his mother's bedroom, he saw her sitting in her chair staring out the window at the snow that had begun to fall.

"You treated her badly. She left you."

"I know. When did she leave?"

"Over an hour ago. She's already on the train on her way back to Lawrenceville. I didn't like her at first, but she's a good woman. She's a good wife for you."

"I know. I love her, and I'm going after her," he said.

His mother glanced up at him. "Good. She's a wonderful woman. So much better than Eloise."

He smiled. "I love Katie, Mom.

"I know, son. Go get her and bring her home. Even if you have to go to Lawrenceville. I'll be fine."

Shocked at his mother's words, he hurried out the door. Never before would his mother have wanted him to leave her for several days, and this time she was telling him to go.

Running out of the house, he pulled loose the reins of his horse and climbed into the saddle. He was going after his wife and confront Frank. The man was not getting away with what he'd done.

Chapter Twelve

Riding into town, Daniel knew the hour was late. All the shops and restaurants were closed and very few people were on the streets. When he rode up in front of the train depot, he saw his horse and buggy. She was gone. Disappointment filled him and with a weary heart he slid off his horse and walked over to the buggy.

He stared at her suitcase sitting in the floorboard and relief flowed through his veins like water. But where was she? Gazing around the town he noticed Frank's office had a light shining from the window. Maybe she went to speak with Frank. Telling him she was leaving.

His heart all but stopped beating at the thought of her being with Frank. The man he had been friends with disappeared, replaced by a conniving man who would harm anyone to get what he wanted. Including his best friend.

Fear for Katie had his feet running across the street, he opened the door and strode into Frank's office. Katie sat tied to a wooden chair, her big green eyes staring at him with fear, shaking her head, her mouth stuffed with a rag.

"What the hell?"

"Stop," Frank demanded. "I hadn't exactly planned on you coming to the party, but maybe it's best this way."

Daniel stared at Frank. "I should warn you that I know everything."

Shaking his head, Frank aimed a gun at Daniel. "You killed the woman I loved. Eloise was leaving you for me. And you pushed her out into the snow."

"No, Frank, I didn't. Jack Edwards, the foreman you recommended, was arrested this afternoon for her death. He was blackmailing her because he saw the two of you together. He opened his mouth and sang like a bird, telling me everything. You hired him after her death to ruin the vineyard."

Frank's face turned red. "You're lying to protect yourself."

"You were having an affair with my wife. She was leaving me to go to you, until Jack killed her," Daniel said, advancing toward Frank. Knowing he had to save Katie, she was an innocent. "You're the one behind the destruction of the vineyard. We were partners. Friends."

Frank's eyes widened. "You killed the woman I loved. I could sell that land for double the value and I have every intention of getting rid of it once I kill you."

"Is it too hard for you to believe you were wrong? That Jack is the killer? He's sitting in jail at this moment, telling the sheriff everything. Including your part in the destruction of the vineyard. Do you want to add murder to your list of crimes as well?"

He waved the gun in his hand at Daniel.

"Shut up! Change of plans. I'm going to kill Katie. I'm going to kill you and make it appear as if you had a lover's quarrel, which everyone in town knows you did. No one will question whether you killed Katie or not," Frank said, walking towards Daniel.

Daniel noticed his shoulder was hanging at an odd angle and blood was oozing down his shirt. "What happened to your shoulder? Looks like someone stabbed you." He lowered his voice. "Remember how we wrestled in college? Remember how I always won?"

Frank's eyes widened and with a scream he lifted the gun.

Seeing the weapon aimed at his chest a spark of fear zinged up Daniel's spine. He dropped and rolled on the floor, slamming into Frank's legs, knocking him down. The gun exploded. Wrestling on the floor, he grabbed Frank's wounded arm, and yanked it behind him while Frank screamed in pain.

Daniel twisted the gun from his hand. Doubling up his fist, he punched him in the face and he slumped unconscious on the ground. When Daniel saw Frank was out, he stood and hurried to Katie. He yanked the cloth from her mouth.

"Are you all right?"

"I'm fine," she said. "So glad to see you. I should never have left you and the vineyard. I should have stayed and fought for you."

Quickly he untied her and then pulled her into his arms. "No, you were right to leave. I'm sorry, Katie. I should never have come in and yelled at you this afternoon. Please forgive me.

"I was wrong to think you were the one doing the damage to the vineyard. I know it was Jack and Frank. When I came home the house was cold and empty without you. I love you, Katie, I want to spend my life with you. Have babies and grow old, please forgive me. Stay and I promise I'll trust you from now until eternity."

She smiled at him and wrapped her arms around him. "I love you, Daniel. Almost as soon as I got to town, I regretted leaving. I love the life we're creating together. I want to be by your side and learn about wine and raise your children."

He smiled at his mail-order bride, his heart filled with warmth.

"I love you Katie Maverick O'Malley. You've stormed into my life and filled it with sunshine and laughter, and please don't ever leave me ever again. I need you."

She laughed. That delightful sound that always made him smile. "I love you, Daniel. I love our vineyard and think we will have a very bright future selling wine and raising grapes and children."

Squeezing her tightly to him, he kissed the tip of her nose and then her lips. "I'm ready to take you home, where you belong."

With a smile she wrapped her arm around his waist and then she pulled back, her eyes widening. "Daniel, I found signed contracts. All they needed was your signature."

"They're invalid. We won't lose the vineyard. I'll never sign."

He closed his eyes. His best friend, a person he considered his brother. Frank's betrayal consumed him, filling him with rage, his stomach clenching. He hated that his best friend, a man he trusted, tried to ruin him.

A noise from behind startled Daniel and as he whirled seeing Frank reaching for the gun. He raised it toward Katie and he stepped in front of her as the gun went off.

The sound of a second shot, surprised him as the bullet slammed into his shoulder and he was falling towards the floor. He slumped onto his wife's soft body, managing to break his fall to keep from hurting her.

Pain radiated from his shoulder as the sheriff rushed into the office. Darkness started to descend and he heard Katie screaming. "No."

~

December 20, 1890

Dear Genny and Julia,
So much has happened since my last letter. I would tell you about the events, but then you would worry about me, so I'm just going to tell you that our home is happy and filled with love.

Even Mother O'Malley has changed and we are good friends. Sometimes there are reasons why people are so angry and I learned she had every reason to be unhappy. But that is all in the past and Daniel and I are so blessed.

I'm expecting our first child sometime in late August. We're both excited and his mother is busy knitting blankets for the little one. I'm thrilled to be starting our family and can't wait to see our child.

Of course, I worry with the death of my family that my child could become an orphan, but I try not to let those thoughts intrude. And even if it happens, I know my mother and father's presence is what guided me. If the worst happens, I will guide this child as well.

I thank the good Lord every day for sending me to Daniel. He's become an excellent husband who I love so very much. Though the first months was extremely rocky, we have now settled the issues and are partners building our wine business, preparing for the future.

May this letter find both of you happy and celebrating the holidays. As always, I miss you and hope if ever you are near, you will spend time at our home. I know with the baby coming, I won't be able to visit you, but someday, my friends, we will be reunited.

As always, I keep you in my prayers and know the factory fire we all hated was a blessing in disguise. Happy holidays to you and yours.

Much love,
Katie

~

New Year's Eve, Daniel stared at the people seated at their dinner table. His wife had once again outdone herself. The atmosphere was happy and everyone was celebrating the holidays.

His shoulder was still bandaged but healing nicely, though his wife would not let him do anything strenuous around the vineyard. But his new foreman had kept things running and came to the house every day to give him a full report on the vines and even the wine.

His mother was happier than she'd been in years. She seemed to be thriving with the company they were now having since he had been completely cleared in Eloise's death. And while he hated that Frank, his best friend had been killed by the sheriff, he couldn't help but think the man he'd been friends with had ceased to exist years ago.

Jack Edwards confessed to killing Eloise and was on trial for her murder. Daniel was relieved to finally put this all behind him, and felt relieved Eloise would receive justice for her premature death.

Next year looked to be the best year the vineyard had to date, but there was something even more exciting to look forward to and he couldn't wait to tell everyone.

He rose from the dinner table and walked over to the chair where his wife sat. He stood in front of her, gazing at her bemused expression. "Thank you all for spending New Year's Eve with my family. My wonderful mother, Betty. Katie, my ray of sunshine, I love so very much and have a surprise for."

He turned her chair to face him. "When you got off the train, I had no intention of marrying you that day. When I look back and think I almost let you go, it frightens me. We had a rushed ceremony and I had no ring. You never even received a proper proposal of marriage from me, just a letter Frank had written."

Sighing he dropped to one knee, pulled the ring box out of his pocket and opened it to a sparkling band with tiny diamonds surrounding an emerald. Katie's eyes widened and her hands flew up to her face. "I want to make it up to you. Katie Maverick O'Malley, will you do me the honor and marry me again, in a church this time?"

She threw her arms around his neck and whispered in his ear. "Of course, I will. And it would be wonderful to have a ceremony with your mother and our friends there. And baby O'Malley growing inside me."

He leaned back and slid the ring on her hand. She kissed him on the lips, as a tear slid down her cheek.

"I love you, Daniel."

He smiled. "Don't ever leave me, Katie, I have more love for you than my heart can hold.

Sighs were heard around the table and several of the women were wiping their eyes, including his mother.

He stood and pulled Katie to her feet. Picking up his wine glass he raised it in the air and everyone followed his example. "A toast to my lovely bride. We've been blessed this year and next year looks to be the best year ever for both our vineyard and our personal lives. My beautiful wife is expecting our first child sometime next summer and I couldn't be happier. To the coming year."

When life looked so very bleak, Frank had brought him Katie, his bright ray of sunlight that had chased away his demons and helped him clear his name. Katie, his American Bride.

Thank You For Reading!

Dear Reader,

Thank you. I know I say this at the end of every book, but I do so because we've just shared an experience together. Without you, my stories would all just be words on paper.

If you enjoyed reading this book, there are 49 more in the series! Find out about the rest of the American Mail-Order Brides here, http://www.newwesternromance.com

As always, if you're inclined, I would appreciate you letting everyone know by leaving a few words on your favorite vendor's website. Whether or not you loved the book or hated it,-I'd enjoy your feedback.

If you enjoy western historical authors, please join the Pioneer Hearts group on Facebook. This is a fabulous group of readers and authors who enjoy westerns. We have lots of fun and there is always something going on.

Sign up for my newsletter if you'd like to learn about my new releases before everyone else.

Thanks for venturing into my world and may I see you here again soon.

Yours in Drama, Divas, Bad Boys and Romance!
Sincerely,

Sylvia McDaniel

Books by Sylvia McDaniel

Contemporary Romance

Standalones
The Reluctant Santa
My Sister's Boyfriend
The Wanted Bride
The Relationship Coach
Her Christmas Lie
Secrets, Lies, and Online Dating
Paying for the Past
Cupid's Revenge

Anthologies
Kisses, Laughter & Love
Christmas with you

Collaborative Series

Magic, New Mexico
Touch of Decadence

Western Historicals

Standalones
A Hero's Heart
A Scarlet Bride
Second Chance Cowboy

The Cuvier Women
Wronged
Betrayed
Beguiled

Lipstick and Lead
Desperate
Deadly
Dangerous
Daring
Determined
Deceived

Scandalous Suffragettes
Abigail
Bella
Callie
Faith

The Burnett Brides
The Rancher Takes a Bride
The Outlaw Takes a Bride
The Marshal Takes a Bride
The Christmas Bride

Anthologies
Wild Western Women
Courting the West
Wild Western Women Ride Again

Collaborative Series

The Surprise Brides
Ethan

American Mail Order Brides
Katie

About the Author

Sylvia McDaniel is a best-selling, award-winning author of historical romance and contemporary romance novels. Known for her sweet, funny, family-oriented romances, Sylvia is the author of The Burnett Brides, a western historical western series, The Cuvier Widows, a Louisiana historical series, and several short contemporary romances.

She is the former President of the Dallas Area Romance Authors, a member of the Romance Writers of America®, and a member of Novelists Inc. Her novel, A Hero's Heart, was a 1996 Golden Heart Finalist. Several other books have placed or won in the San Antonio Romance Authors Contest and the LERA Contest, and she was a Golden Network Finalist.

Married for nearly twenty years to her best friend, they

have two dachshunds that are beyond spoiled and a good-looking, grown son who thinks there's no place like home. She loves gardening, shopping, knitting, and football (Cowboys and Bronco's fan), but not necessarily in that order.

Look for her the first Tuesday of every month at the Plotting Princesses blogspot, and be sure to sign up for her newsletter to learn about new releases and contests. Every month a new subscriber is entered into a drawing for a free book!

She can be found online at: www.sylviamcdaniel.com or on Facebook. You can write to Sylvia at P.O. Box 2542, Coppell, TX 75019.

Looking for a new book to read?

The trouble with identical twins…

He's back. The one guy she never wanted to see again. Her high school indiscretion, Brent Moulton, has returned to Tyler, Texas. Only Jennifer Riley knows the truth about that night so long ago when she switched places with her twin sister, Julie, and gave her virginity along with her heart, to her sister's boyfriend in the backseat of his father's Mustang.

…they look alike.

Fifteen years later, life has thrown them back together. Will Brent realize he slept with the wrong twin? Will he overcome his commitment issues and realize that Jennifer just might be the right twin for him.

Sneak Peek into My Sister's Boyfriend

"Never again," Jennifer Riley, vowed as she stepped into the black-paneled, wooden coffin outside the entrance to the Hilton Hotel in downtown Tyler, Texas. Lying down inside the macabre structure, she could hear traffic whiz by on Main Street.

She tugged at the filmy black, chiffon dress, trying to cover as much of her exposed cleavage as possible. "No matter how busy Julia gets, or how much she pleads, I refuse to do this again. I didn't come back to Tyler to portray the over-the-hill sex queen."

Paul, her sister's employee, stood quietly by, holding the lid open. "Ready?"

Jennifer took a deep breath, dreading the darkness that would engulf her. "Yes, make it quick. I hate lying inside this creepy box."

Jennifer watched the coffin lid come down, shutting out the noise and headlights from the traffic.

"You all right?" Paul called.

"Hurry!" Her breath sounded harsh in the darkness. She felt the pallbearers lift the coffin onto the cart and roll it along the sidewalk into the hotel.

After tonight, Julia, her twin sister, would have to find someone else to jump out of coffins and sing seductively when she needed help with her business. No ifs, ands, or buts!

As the new Development Director at County General Hospital, Jennifer would be way too busy to fill in as backup for her sister's fledgling singing telegram business. Not to mention that popping out of coffins could be damaging to her new career.

The cart jostled along the hallway of the hotel, until she heard wolf whistles and loud, boisterous, voices cheering and she knew they'd arrived at the party.

Paul rapped on the coffin lid. "Are you ready?"

Jennifer cleared her throat and searched for the button that would pop open the door. Whatever happened to women jumping out of cakes? What nut case thought coffins were funny?

The coffin lifted. She gripped the sides, trying to find her balance as they slid the casket off the cart until the box stood upright. She landed with a thunk on the floor, jarring her. You just couldn't get good pallbearers anymore.

Paul tapped on the side of the coffin three times to let her know it was time.

"In honor of your birthday, your friends and family have given you a gift from the other side. The other side of the hill, that is," Paul announced, as the noise from the crowd swelled.

Music started to play and Jennifer hit the button on the inside of the wooden box. The door sprang open and she slinked out, the chiffon dress clinging like a second skin that left little to the imagination.

"Happy Birthday…" she sang in her alto voice, her eyes blinded by the lights. She blinked rapidly, hoping her eyesight would adjust to the brightness of the room. When her vision finally cleared, she found herself staring into the face of the one man she'd hoped never to see again.

There before her, wearing a stunned expression on his face and a Marvin The Martian, child's birthday hat, sat Brent Moulton.

"Well, I'll be damned," said the captain of her old high school football team, the person voted 'most handsome' and 'most likely to succeed.'

Jennifer's voice cracked as she gazed into the emerald eyes of the boy she'd secretly dreamed of. A lock of dark hair lay across his high forehead. His full lips smiled as she stumbled over the words to the song she'd sung countless times.

I should never have agreed to do this tonight!

Dancing for a man who, almost fifteen years ago, hadn't known the difference between her and Julia was anything but special, but the show had to go on.

She slinked around him, her heart beating in her throat as she ran her hands along the hard contoured muscles of his shoulders during her act. Brent must have existed on nothing but Wheaties in college, because his physique resembled a professional football player's, rather than that of the high school kid of her dreams.

Of course, he would never remember her. She had portrayed Julia that night so long ago, when they'd pulled a switch on him. Nevertheless, deep down inside, the foolish young girl she'd been back then had convinced herself that he knew who she was, and to her, their identity seemed apparent. Yes, Jennifer and Julia looked alike, but when you really knew the two of them, their differences were obvious.

With a coo that she hoped resembled Christina Aguilera, she ran her fingers down his cheek as she began the last chorus of the song, the place in the act where she leaned forward and placed a chaste kiss on his cheek. She gazed at his lips, full and inviting, and remembered the feel of them against her own that moonlit night when he believed he was kissing Julia's lips.

She chickened out.

As the song ended, Brent reached up and unexpectedly pulled her onto his lap, wrapping her in his muscular arms.

A full-blown explosion of magnetism rushed at Jennifer like a Eurail locomotive as she gazed into his laughing emerald eyes, catching her completely off guard.

Fifteen years had passed since that night, and still he'd tag-teamed her libido and brought back all those annoying yearnings she thought long ago buried.

Brent sat holding her sprawled across his lap, her heart beating a sharp rhythm against her chest. Hopefully, he'd forgotten his date with 'Julia' the night before they left for college.

He ran his hand down her arm, leaving a trail of goose bumps beneath the black chiffon sleeve of her dress. "Hi," he said as his gaze swept down the length of her, his voice deeper, sexier than she remembered.

"Hi," she managed as a shiver ran down her spine and her lungs tightened beneath the unyielding black dress.

"It's been a long time." The corner of his lips turned up in a cocky grin. "Shouldn't I get some kind of official birthday kiss?"

www.ingramcontent.com/pod-product-compliance
Lightning Source LLC
Chambersburg PA
CBHW071827190726
48292CB00005B/1648